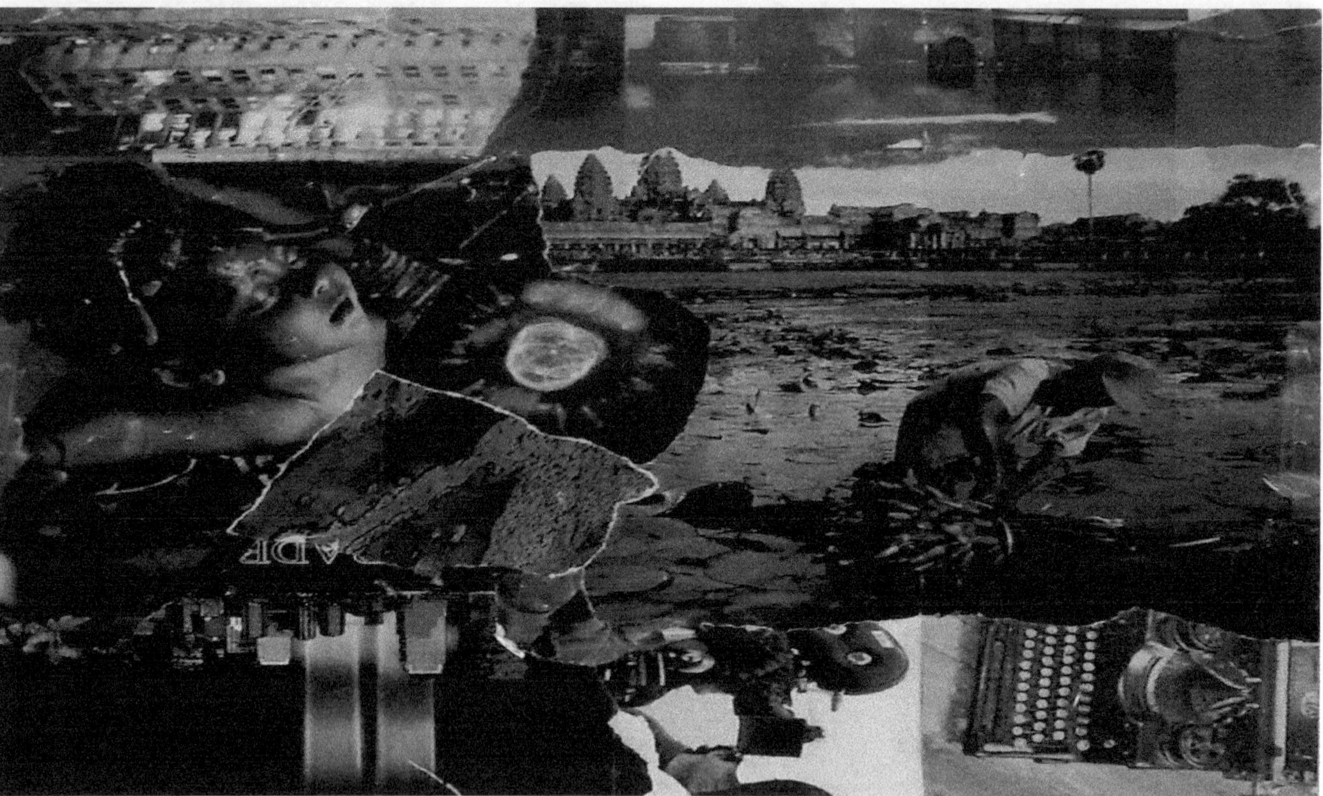

Exist.

OTHER KOKOPELLIMA PRESS BOOKS BY ANGEL BRYNNER

Eutaxis   Ecclesia   Exodus

Erebus   Exist   Esthesis   Epicharis

Elision   Elysum   Empyrean

AOLAB active art decks & books BY ANGEL BRYNNER

ZION   HALCYON   DELUGE   BLOOD OF MY BLOOD

FLESH OF MY FLESH   BONE OF MY BONE

BLACKWATER   OVERFLOW   EDEN   ZENITH

AOLAB Travelogues BY ANGEL BRYNNER

BOTTOM OF THE NINTH WARD BULLETINS

BLACKWATER RISING

Anthologies BY ANGEL BRYNNER

FIRESTARTER   FIREWALKER

Grievechronic Revisionist AOLAB Active-Art books by Angel Brynner

DELUGE, ZION, HALCYON BLOOD FLESH& BONE ZENITH

Exist.

/grievechronic\

Angel Brynner

KOKOPELLIMA PRESS
MIAMI   NEW ORLEANS
KOKOPELLIMAPRESS.COM

Library of Congress
Cataloging-in-Publication Data
Brynner, Angel
Exist, grievechronic/ Angel Brynner
Library of Congress control number:2019956724

Audiobook edition
ISBN: 978-1-950077-40-3
Copyright © 2026 Angel Brynner

First edition
ISBN:978-1-950077-00-7
Copyright © 2007 Angel Brynner

Cover and book design by AOLAB. Additional artwork credit:
MACROVECTOR/FREEPIK, 4045/FREEPIK| FREEPIK AI

KOKOPELLIMA PRESS
MIAMI   NEW ORLEANS
KOKOPELLIMAPRESS.COM

Exist.

For the wild Love that God had cover me
all the way, even after all gone through.

And for every "Christian" who helped this
get here on time.

There exists a place
where we can escape the
 nightmares of life,
A peace in the madness
that must be entered
to meet the ones within us
capable of our highest crimes
and lowest glories.

You can't overcome
the demons in your past
until you make peace with
 the strange beauty housed within it.

chapter one

Anukai reached the riverbank and looked around. The air smelled of little boy and rose petals.

"And peanut butter," she said, wrinkling her nose. Suddenly she heard soft snoring.

She tiptoed over, parted the reeds and found him asleep on the floor on other side of the looking glass, a plate of cookies next to his head and the remnants of peanut butter pie smeared across his face. She looked over her shoulder then slid her hand through.

Gabryl woke with a jump as she tried to come through the mirror. He took hold of her hand and pulled her across. She shyly dusted at the crumbs on his face.

"What took you so long?" he whispered."I almost thought-" "I said I wasn't going to forget-" she shyly whispered back.

They sat and stared at each other sheepishly for a long time after finally exchanging names, then ate cookies in silence on his nest of bedding on the floor.

Anukai motioned to his chest."-Show me." she said simply.
"But it's going to-" he started nervously.
"It won't hurt-" she tried to assure him.
"But-" he said hesitantly.

"Do you want me to get them out or not?" She sighed. They didn't have much time.

"Look- this isn't easy-" His voice quaked.

"coward , punk, bastard, fag, crybaby-" started to crest inside of him and show up as finely printed welts of shame on his

skin.

"I'm sorry-" she whispered and grabbed his hand.

He turned away and looked out the window. It had begun raining. Guilt plastered itself across her face from having hurt him. She shook nervously, refusing the thoughts shooting at her from inside as the bad words she was always called rose to the surface of her own skin.

"beast, ogre, ugly, monster-"

She shut her eyes angrily against them and made them fall into a tiny heap on the floor. "I – I just want to help- I can't take you until you show me-"

He looked at the pile of bad words on the floor at her feet in confusion, humiliated. "It's going to hurt-" he wailed softly, grabbing at his scarred chest through his t-shirt, not caring for the first time ever if anyone saw him cry. "Every time I look at it, it starts to hurt all over again and I can't breathe, and-" The bad names rang so loudly in his head that she could hear them. She wrapped around him as he trembled until the names he had taken in fell off too. He started to calm down, tucking his head under her chin as he pressed his wet face into her chest.

"I promise you it's not going to hurt." She whispered. " I know it sounds like it will-it even sounded like it would to me when He first told me about it-

"But when it happened," his voice hitched, "it hurt so bad that- I just don't ever wanna feel that again-"

It was raining even harder outside. The Angels around them stroked her hair gently to help her remember what to say. It came out of her mouth hesitantly.

"...Remember when you washed my hair and you promised me

it wouldn't hurt? I cried because I didn't believe you-

because of how she used to hurt me when she did it- but after I let you do it she never was able to hurt me again... because I believed in you- in here- and I knew that hurt was all her out there. I trusted you." Anukai gently cupped her hands on his chest. "Now...*you* trust me so these can't hurt you no more either-" They peered at each other in the half-light of the room.

Nervously, Gabryl laid back down on the blankets and closed his eyes. He crossed his little arms over his stomach, slowly pulled the tee-shirt up over his head and tucked it behind his shoulders.

His body shook, he couldn't hear anything but the pounding of his heart in his ears and his teeth chattering inside his head. Apprehensively, he opened one eye.

Anukai's head hung over him. She softly cried over the rough scars that wrapped around his chest as if he'd been ripped open with a cat of nine tails. A tiny groan escaped from her mouth as tears slid through the air between them and landed on his chest, creating a ripple on contact as if Gabryl was a small pond.

Gabryl looked around at his room shape-shifting as the ripple spread across his ribcage.

He blinked in confusion. When he opened his eyes he was on the ground in a forest flooded with light. Anukai peered into his face with concern waiting for him to breathe.

"What the-" he wheezed. She happily threw her arms around his neck.

Mystified, Gabryl took in the cathedral of trees that surrounded them. Between blinks he saw what looked like spider-webs full of colorful scraps of paper pieced together that shifted into vistas of whole worlds, then back again to webs.

"Is this-where you-hide- when...?" he whispered as he tattooed everything he could about the space into his memory.

She nodded shyly and crawled back from him, hiding behind her hair." But...want to see who I'm going to become anyway?"

Gabryl nodded sheepishly. They pulled each other up and walked through a tiny hallway of trees into a clearing filled with gigantic paintings of her, inlaid with gold and silver. Fabrics glistened in the paintings like they'd give if he brushed his fingers against them. Her skin, a different shade in every portrait, pulsed with joy. The irises faded to white and back again with gentle breezes that seemed to blow through the images out into the clearing, which made the tufts, coils and textures of hair in each picture undulate like leaves on a tree. Everything seemed to have extra ounces of life that begged to be seen, touched and taken in.

Anukai reached up and gently closed Gabryl's gaping mouth. When he looked at her in amazement she let out a peal of laughter.

"How did you-" he started, "They move! And they-"

Anukai shrugged her shoulders shyly. "I've been doing it for a while," she whispered conspiratorially, " but I hid them Because... I know they'd destroy them all if they found them here..." her voice trailed off.

chapter two

Kagome and Diaz were curled around each other in the trees above the little boy and girl.

Kagome's hair waved gently, the scraps of paper tangled in it refracting prisms of multicolored light across the floor of the forest. She smiled tenderly as the child's secret world came into view for someone else other than her.

Diaz's breath hitched softly as he watched the crayon-scrawled scraps of cardboard Anukai had shown him become masterpieces of color and life when looked at by this little friend of hers that was somehow so familiar to him.

He looked over and stroked Kagome's face affectionately, giving more and more of his life back to her in the silence of the leaves. The color that had only recently returned to him deposited itself along the line of her cheek and danced up into her hairline.

She sighed from the sensation of his touch as she clocked the perimeter. The Punishers had moved in another direction. The two continued to love on one another quietly up in the trees.

chapter three

"I can do something special too," Gabryl whispered softly to Anukai as he tried his best to sit still.

Anukai darkened the hollows of his face with soot to make him look the way she saw him in her head for the picture. Stripes of war paint streaked down his cheeks from when she'd stood behind him and pulled her wet fingers down towards his jaw in her mind. His head was wrapped in scraps of brightly colored fabric and a cape of tiger skins hung down his back on red silk ribbons. He sat before her proudly, feathers and freshly torn leaves tucked behind his ears as if he were a bird-king.

His pants were rolled up to expose his tiny, ashy calves and feet that peeked out from under folds of red plaid cloth the two of them had coiled around him, his tee-shirt still tucked absently behind his shoulders. He looked like a young Masai prince, only honey-colored, strangely tropical, like a barbarian monarch. Tiny strands of colorful beads and gold draped down his chest.

" ...Do you want to see it?" Gabryl asked out of the corner of his mouth so she could finish his portrait and add it to her special gallery. She looked up from her drawing and stared pensively at his forehead as if she'd lost something.

The white dots he'd carefully painted around her eyes on top of the yellow ochre he'd smeared from her cheeks to her temples glinted in the hallowed light and pulled his eyes towards hers.

" ...Do you want to see?" he croaked again, overwhelmed by things he couldn't wrap his head around, unable to stop looking at the image of him reflected in her eyes that let him know she saw him as strong and proud instead of any of the other names he was usually called. "Nevermind," he whispered shyly, stunned by how her eyes saw him.

Anklets jingled with each move she made. The necklaces he'd piled on her swayed in the sweet air as she tried to remember not to suck on the bottom lip he'd so painstaking painted a red line down the center of. The feathered headdress she wore pushed her hair up off of her face into a bushy Mohawk that trailed down her back. He had wrapped her in a sarong of goldenrod plaid Kente cloth and twisted a contrasting scrap of orange, blue and green plaid with brown and white mudcloth that he'd tied across her distended stomach into a big bow at her back. Jade bracelets clinked as Anukai made a few more lines before she put her crayons that melted into paints down.

"No, I wanna see, okay? But first-we have to finish this-" Anukai said softly and pointed at his chest. "Does it hurt or itch now?" she asked.

He shook his head in surprise. It was the longest his wound had not been on his mind that he could remember. He looked down at the skin stretched across his rib-cage, still moist from where her tears had fallen what felt like forever ago. She gently shoved him back onto the grass. The renditions of her wished-for life leaned forward, almost toppling out of their gilt frames to watch.

"No-" he said.

"Good." she whispered. Brightly colored birds flew overhead. His head spun as the forest fell away in spurts, like he was being pulled down a drain.

He lifted up just in time to see her lowering the sapphire crusted handle of a dagger she had pulled from her obi towards him in a trance. "What the-" he hoarsely cried out as her right arm shot out and pinned his neck to the ground.

"Don't move!" she hissed, "you'll make me miss!"
"Stop! What are you doing?!" Gabryl screamed as the blade slammed into his chest, which was now the consistency of clay. She quickly covered his mouth as blackened blood frothed up out of his sternum.

He whimpered, eyes watering in anger as he tried to make his arms fight back but couldn't.

"Shush, it's infected! Stop squirming- Do you even feel it?" Anukai hissed pointedly, her eyes whited out like the ones she had painted on the beings that now crowded around them full of concern.

Gabryl paused. He tried to feel pain, but there was none. He wrinkled his brows in relief and confusion. The renditions of herself sighed with relief and made their ways back to their respective frames of reference.

"Good. Now let me finish." Anukai ordered softly. She slowly slid her hand into the cut she'd made in his chest and pulled out a blackened heart like a well-seasoned Aztec priest.

She held the heart of darkness up to the light and peered at it, confused by how it looked bigger, different than she'd imagined it would. Gabryl's eyes rolled back in his head as he started to black out.

A droplet of his infected blood trickled along her forearm and danced across her bracelets towards the ground in hyper-slow motion. Soon as the infected blood hit the dirt it was as if a flare shot up into the sky.

Little Anukai looked up horror as the ocular force of the Punishers suddenly turned their way. She shook some of the gunk from the little boy's heart, rammed it back in his chest, yanked him up and yelled "The DragonLion!!!Run!"

Instantly, what looked like a cross between a giant metallic Chinese Dragon and a shaggy Chinese Lion appeared in front of them and roared.

Lil Anukai and Gabryl shot off into the trees, running for their lives through the woods towards the river. The echoing jingle of their anklets disrupted Sector's surveillance through the Badlands.

chapter four

At the sound of the flare Kagome jumped up, sending a wave through the veil of hair that was cloaking the kids, her and Diaz up in the trees."Shit!" She snapped.

"Incoming!" Diaz snarled as they leapt out of the tree. Kagome went straight for the portrait of her and him and touched it, turning it back into a cardboard scrawl before tearing it in two.

"What the- what are you doing?!" Diaz yelled.
"I'm saving her life!" she snarled "I know what I'm doing-"
"You're destroying her-"

" *She isn't supposed to be here*- you keep forgetting that! It's what got her into this mess in the first place- YOU and I aren't even supposed -" Kagome seethed, aggravated.

Spiritually wounded, his color began to drain from her all over again. He looked where he knew the Punishers were bound to come. "Don't make this about me and you Kagome! What I-"

"Are you going to help me DO this or are you going to cause more problems?" She snapped evenly.

"What the-" Vayo Kahn Diaz tried to argue back but she cut him off.

"Look-Mr. I Can't crossover~ because all Hell breaks out when I do...what the Fuck are you going to do?" Kagome snarled.

Exasperated, he rolled his eyes. "I'm Not trying to-" He felt her glare get hotter. "Okay- Look-"

Kagome glared and folded her arms over her chest.

Diaz continued. "Look- their retinues are never big enough to handle more than one thing at a time." he hissed. " They obviously were already here hunting me. We can cloak the two of them."

Kagome twisted her lips up in doubt as he continued. "Think about it- you know how one track the Punishers are- and Imagine If they pick up your fugitive ass, alongside the quake of an AWOL me? The rote Directionals they rely on will fry-"

"Ooh! And we can split the ranks before they get it together to Sector up to the Emp for back-up and burn the entire Leuce down." Kagome growled appreciatively. "Welcome the Fuck back, Vayo-" She grunted.

The consorts glowered, roughly kissed and bit down on each other's lips to draw blood that they spat on the ground to cover up the boy's.

Diaz and Kagome frantically kicked up dust over the supernatural spread of it across the paddock, marking the area like a giant x. They whirled around and yanked the last paintings down. The paintings morphed back to scraps of cardboard when they hit the ground as Kagome and Diaz ran into the Leuce after the kids.

chapter five

The collective spirit of the Punishers turned 180 degrees and howled as it pounded across the Badlands in waves towards the bloodletting.

The sickening odor of iron was thick as they materialized in the burning fields. It fought against the stink of sulphur that seeped out of their tar-coated, metallic skins as flames danced across streaks of them, relaxing dense tufts of hair that stuck out the back of helmets worn high on their heads. Facial hair was as painstakingly burnt onto one cheek as it seemed roughly removed on the other side of the same face. Tiny sprays of spit ran after faces that shifted from side to side as eyes heavily fringed with iridescent lashes flashed, the Punishers speaking to each other telepathically.

Their bodies contorted the way things danced in shadows and fire, flickering in response to the solidification of more of their entourage alongside them and the confusion of the matter at hand.

One of the Punishers sniffed the air, bewildered. *"Wait- this makes NO sense- What is that...stench?"*

"... It can't be-" another of the Punishers choked as black smoke trailed out of the corner of the side of his mouth clamped down onto a burning branch of palo santo.

"Make no mistake- That~ is Flesh... Fresh-flesh-! And the blood of Innocents-" snorted the most brutally crafted Punisher to his brethren. His spirit pawed at the air like a forcibly restrained animal even as he tried to stand still.

"It's impossible! This is the Leuce! Flesh can't face this atmosphere-"

"Two impossible signals-yes- but make no mistake..."

chapter six

Positioned between the two children and the actual Punishers on the ground, Diaz took the lead while Kagome bobbed and weaved erratically, creating giant webs of hair through the trees to trap or at least slow down the collective spirit of the Punishers already tracking the children.

Overhead, shards of light broke through the resplendent darkness of the Leuce as Diaz caught his breath and looked back at a furious-faced Kagome.

She swung through the branches spooling traps, her partially cloaked strands of hair infinitely sprawled out behind her like the web encased in a cicada's wing. She caught up and dangled from the trees above him, admiring her work.

"But what about her and the boy?" Diaz started.

"If we do this right, their hands will be too full with us to even remember the flare-" she whispered, the twisted smile of an apex predator splayed across her lips. "Or at least with me- Who knows what's left in you after being blanked so many times?" she chuckled.

"And if it goes wrong?" Diaz smirked, ignoring her jibe.

Kagome's ghostly face darkened. "Then they'll learn the hard way that we were really *protecting* them...from her." Kagome whispered.

"What are you talking about? She's just a kid-" Diaz started.

"Diaz...That beautiful little *child* compelled-" Kagome started then corrected herself.

"No- outright made you-YOU- Mr. Master Builder himself-

Jump into the Badlands in broad, red light...from, of all places, the Arrivals Zone- the most heavily guarded Zone in the Empyrean! And that's *after* Making you bring her up into *that* supposedly impenetrable zone in the first place. Again...and again-" Kagome blushed with pleasure as the truth of what she intimated sunk into Vayo Kahn Diaz.

"Even I can't help but bow down to her and I won't even submit to you-" she continued. " I have absolutely no worries about her handling her business if backed into a corner." Kagome chuckled grimly.

"Yeah... well, she is still a kid- she shouldn't have to handle Any of this-" Diaz grunted protectively like the true guardian of the child he was. "...let's make sure she doesn't have to. Come on-"

Vayo Kahn Diaz sniffed the air and motioned to the southwest, where he sensed the little girl was. Kagome spun over his head and back as she continued to bob and weave through the trees.

chapter seven

A Punisher looked up from his particular set of specialized scanning artillery." *There are shifting breaches into the sands of the Badlands from different directions-"*

"Plus...possibly...Brethren,you won't believe this- I think that's the pattern of the Most-wanted-" he paused, narrowing all of his eyes as he peered back at his machinery to be sure.

"The Fugue?! It can't be- The Fury has not-"

"On top of the Fire in the Hole- which apparently is...the signal Sector sent us in blindly to retrieve-"

"The Fire in the Hole was the - The Master Builder?!"

"The LightBringer?! They sent just Us in after That-?! This is- Cell Suicide!"

Code-named ANC2s by the Denizens above, the re-routed members of the Androgenic Nephilim Cossack Collective were the first beings blotted out before the complexities discerning the difference between a metaphysical mutiny and a mystical misdemeanor had been clarified in the Empyreanic purification processes instituted by the Tryage rulers.

On autopilot by exoskeletons that clamped down into their flesh, twos had been fused into All in Ones without choice, the concept of a blank slate taken literally by the Tryage. Freedman status erased, they'd been re-wired into little more than vicious henchmen at the beginning of Tryage reign in the highest High of Heaven, kept alive for one thing only- putting out fires. Tattoos crested down the side of one Punisher body as metallic needles penitently studded the pristine, numbed flesh of the being trapped in the exoskeleton alongside it.

Coils of copper spun clockwise on fingers to synch the retinue to one another as well as pace themselves against the mission at hand. The air in front of them waved from the intense heat emanating off of them while trickles of carbon dioxide wafted up out of nostrils and mouths.

They specialized in straight-out snuff-outs of the Spiritual sort but this time...they'd unknowingly been sent into the blazes of the Badlands to quietly retrieve the most dangerous fire-starter of them all, Master Builder Vayo Kahn Diaz. Before any more of the less docile denizenry caught a whiff of his energetic absence. Not that they would've had say in deflecting the directive. The Punishers had no leader. They were only equipped to follow orders.

The Punishers began to sweat as the next possible moves whirled off of tongues in discordant harmony. The peripheral thought of patching into the Empyrean Sector to report made synapses collapse on themselves, which would lead to them simply being snuffed out by a cell similar to their own.

"Bring the fire in the hole back...Now." was the order we were sent out on," some of the Punishers muttered in agreement, but not enough for consensus.

They all knew of yet were not equipped to speak on the window retrieval slammed shut, the silent disappearances connected to the crazy leaps fires in holes took to snuff themselves out of the Highest High, nor the brimstoned state the Punishers dragged them back to the Empyrean reeling from, as ordered.

But the bittersweet smell of spilled blood in the heart of the Leuce overrode set courses and battered their caged senses.

"*What do we do?Fire, Fugue, Flesh...or Blood?*" The Punishers pressed all members of the cell to make the call.

"*One hail of stone. Come what may. Dragonlion is on the Flesh. We begin with the blood.*"

The Punishers slammed down their helmets in unison and flickered in the shadows as they evaporated in pursuit.

chapter eight

Due to contact with the infected blood of the little boy as it mixed with the supernatural blood of Kagome and Diaz and soaked into the ground, the future selves of Anukai reanimated in the clearing. They hid under the cardboard as the slabs morphed back into paintings and streaked the bizarre mix of bloodied mud below them all over their skins like war paint.

The Punisher cell began to materialize. Renditions of Anukai all grown up trembled under overturned gilt-frames as the monsters known for setting fires in the Leuce motioned towards the paintings, pushing their helmets up in sync to get better views as they pressed into the ring of trees.

"What is this?"
"...doesn't matter- Destroy it-"

A Punisher moved towards a painting and roughly knocked the frame over to get a better look anyway. The Mother Anukai imagined she'd one day be knelt in the bloody grove over the huddled bodies of her two children and bared her teeth up at it.

"What the-" the Punisher stammered as the family swarmed it with all their might. Metallic red blood spewed out of it as the Punisher collapsed under the brute force of them. Another Punisher roughly yanked one of the feral kids off of its comrade by the throat and held him over the head of the mother as the child swung at the monster.

"Beg for his life!" the Punisher hissed and slashed the little boy's throat before she could even open her mouth.

Bedlam exploded in the clearing as The Punishers and the Reflections of Anukai's future Selves went equally berserk.

Punishers ripped open the backs of paintings and massacred fugitives and transgressors with as much force as delinquent aspects of Anukai's future spirit effectively assaulted the Punishers.

Their bare hands slipped through the flesh of the Punisher cell like they were coated with corrosive acid due to war paint the splinters of Anukai re-upped on each time their bodies slammed into the ground, making the actuality of their touch as powerful as the weaponry of the Punishers.

One of the Punishers screamed as the Bride violently rammed her bloodied fist through its chest. He collapsed to the ground before she could extract her hand and took her with him into the grassy gore the war was waged on. Her white dress soaked up the slain aspects of herself as she ripped herself free and bit into one side of the face of the Punisher, headlocking the caged monster and ramming her hand through his jaw to grab at both of his tongues and yank them out of his head.

"Retreat!!!!"

The few Punishers a hand above in the battle helmeted up and dematerialized, aimed towards the original target.

The Bride got up and dragged the Punisher carcass to the center of the clearing, looking around unsteadily to see if any other aspects of herself needed help. She saw the corpse of her future groom and crumpled to the ground. No one else was left.

The Dreams of Anukai died alongside the groans of monsters whose only reason to be had been to snuff them out, but those dreams died victoriously because they had finally put up a fight and won. The wails of the bewildered Punishers was music to their ears.

Brightly colored birds nestled alongside black crows and brown speckled sparrows in the trees. They waited until the last breath went up, then descended to feast like the carrion they were.

chapter nine

Kagome and Diaz looked at the sky then down at the dirt.

Kagome's eyes were wild from the smell of spilt Punisher blood in the air, and it took all of Diaz's energy to keep her focused because she was magnetically pulled by it.

"I love you, Kago-" Diaz whispered as he slit his wrist and let the last of this batch of blood drop to the ground and catch fire.

"...more than you know, Dio-" she whispered back as she followed suit. They smeared each other's blood across themselves as their so-called lives drained out and cloaked like ghosts in the trees, laying in wait for their bloodletting to be hooked onto.

chapter ten

Anukai and Gabryl ran as fast as they could, their skin scratched by branches as if the terrain was fighting against them.

Headdresses and necklaces were ripped from them as they stumbled in the dark. Anukai tripped over a fallen log and fell head-first into mud. She started to cry as Gabryl crouched over her and frantically prodded her forward, both of them on their hands and knees in the mud.

The tracking hologram of the beast roared behind them as they crawled lower and lower to the ground until they were totally coated with mud on their bellies. The little girl started to shake with fear and she rolled over onto her back as her eyes began to flicker in the dark. Gabryl held his finger up to her lips to shush her. He closed her eyes as he slid next to her on the ground and wiped at some of the muck on her face with his own mud-caked hand, inadvertently depositing more where clean skin had been. The hologram of the Chinese Dragonlion abruptly stopped a few yards away from them and roared as the signal of the two disappeared.

Anukai's eyes popped back open to all white as they slithered on their backs in the direction of the river, never looking away from the confounded Dragonlion that was barely thirty paces behind them, still attempting to scan the area and pick up the scent it somehow lost.

chapter eleven

The handful of Punishers that had barely escaped the bride's brawl in the grove condensed a few yards behind the hologram of Dragonlion as it disappeared from sight.

They pushed up their helmets and peered into the dark of the wood towards the river.

As soon as one of the Punishers made a tentative step in the direction of the children, the trees that had been fighting to keep their little bodies under wraps let through a breeze full of the fiery smell of Master Builder Vayo Kahn Diaz.

The Punishers motioned towards him with their ringed fingers in unison, slammed back down their headgear and vaporized just beyond the mud-caked exposed toes of Anukai and Gabryl.

They gasped, sprung up and ran like wildfire towards the river, never looking back.

Two lone Punishers appeared in the trees where the others

had first touched down, their brethren nowhere to be found. They followed the kids, heads down low to the ground.

chapter twelve

Diaz nodded to Kagome as his spirit blended into the shadows of bark, mud and moss. When the clutch of Punishers came to the small clearing he uncloaked at the base of a tree, smiling broadly.

"Gentlemen!" Diaz boomed, "...and then some," he purred in deference to the feminine forcibly fused within their cages.

"So nice of you to join me- I was waiting for you! The Badlands are a bore this leap, such a disappointment- "

The Punishers looked at one another and back at him warily. There was no way it could be this easy. Their eyes had to be playing tricks on them.

"Don't look so surprised-" He whispered up at them. "You're Cossacks, Blanked Originals... ANC$_2$s on autopilot..." he sneered as he slowly stood, "and ANC$_2$s...by definition are too smart to be surprised by jumpy ole me." Vayo Kahn Diaz grinned. "Now take me in," he spat.

The Punishers looked around, still shaken by the surprise of the battle they'd all but fled, desperately in need of someone, anyone, to take the lead.

"Fine, fine ...let me add to that...that's an order! Now do it!"

As if magnetized by the tone of authority in his voice the gaggle of Punishers clumsily stepped towards him to do as commanded. Kagome swooped down behind them and ripped off a glyph-crusted Katana blade from the hip of one.

The Punishers whipped around just in time to see her jump up into the trees and leap over and down in front of Diaz.

They spun back around in shock.

"Ok, ok- Now your shock at that? Makes more sense~ poor things. Then again, with your kind hunting her down again & again, killing the good in her until only the bad was left at the wheel...there's only so much pity your fear deserves." he snarled softly. Kagome smiled sweetly and raised a brow as her monocle floated up over her ear and positioned itself in front of her eye.

The Punishers reeked of terror due to being face to face with the Fury called the Fugue under breaths throughout the ANC ranks. She had decimated more Punisher cells sent out on missions in the Badlands than there were cells left in the employ of the Empyrean with no explanation, as if for nothing but sport. And no directives from above in response to her murderous activity ever manifested.

"But I understand...this b- she can go a lil nuts sometimes, no?" Diaz chuckled, the laughter never reaching his eyes.

"Dia~"Kagome growled softly.
"Yeah, bay?" Diaz murmured back affectionately.

"Did...did you just almost call me a-" Kagome said through gritted teeth. Blade raised, she was ready to slice through anything that made the slightest wrong move, in front or behind her, Punisher or otherwise. An almost imperceptible flutter of nervousness skidded across the surface of Diaz, who'd forgotten her...issues with certain words.

"No! No-no- Honey, I – what I was trying to get across to my audience-" he chuckled skittishly as he made the universal sign language for *flippin crazy* behind her back for the Punishers, who were even more on edge than he now was.

"Because you know," she said, the smile never leaving her lips, "That I'd off you not blinking an eye just like these Mothaf-"

"Bayh-I -I didn't call you a-" Diaz stammered angrily.

"But you were about to, weren't you? For Effect!Admit it!" Kagome screeched.
"Kago, look-what I was trying to say-"
"B?! What the hell were you going to say, Dia? Huh?! What the F else does B begin Diaz? Butterfly?! You were gonna call me an fn-" her voice went up an Octave.

"Can we stay focused on the thing at hand?" he fussed.

"Oh, now you're telling me where my focus needs to-?!" Kagome yelled hotly. "You shouldn't even be here- this is my territory! These are MY Food! And what am I doing, the first time I see your jumpy ass in like beyond eons?! I'm standing here, some beast of burden's pretty-assed fn blade in my hands, protecting you! About to slay like it ain't been slain- over your interloping, no idea if he's coming or goin Ass! And you're almost calling me a B~itch?! In front of my prey?!" She hissed belligerently.

"I'm- this is MY zone!Do you hear me?! You are stirring up shit my zone doesn't Need !" Kagome screamed maniacally.

Vayo Kahn Diaz and the Punishers stepped back from her in unison like she was about to blow, hands on all weaponry present just in case she detonated and destroyed them all.

"Are you Freaking kidding me?!" Diaz howled defensively. "If You would've kept you ass at home a loooooong time ago, none of this would be happening now!" He yelled at the back of her head.

Kagome cocked her head to the side. "I should've stayed at home?!" she roared. Her head clicked a quarter- inch to her left to catch a bewildered Diaz as he inched farther away from her. "I can't believe you just said that," she whispered.

"Kagome- I-" he whispered harshly as his eyes flicked towards two of the Punishers who inched forward as she looked away.

All expression left her face as Kagome shrugged her shoulders and the katana sliced through the heavenly vocal cords of one Punisher before it made contact with the underbelly of the other. Sacred blood gushed out and splattered onto the feet of the rest of the shocked cell, the first time the Punishers had seen one of their own killed by weapons they'd forged themselves. She blushed and licked at a spray of the blood that had landed on her cheek. Her color returned as her eyes rolled back in her head. A deranged look slowly fluttered across her face.

"Kagome-" Diaz whispered, "...weren't we going to do this differently?" he asked gently, trying to remain calm so the smell of his fear would not encourage the Berserker the taste of too much blood could easily awaken. "I mean...Together?"

"Oh yeah," she murmured, "together-" as a clarified sweet smile rose again.

"There are five of us left to the two of them" shot across the collective consciousness of the still standing Punishers as they tried to ignore the two bleeding out into the Leuce at their feet.

Diaz rolled his eyes. "That's right, FIVE!" he yelled impatiently, "I can hear you! But as Master Builder, eons above you in rank I gave you an order a ways back that you have yet to obey! I said take me in! Do it! Now!"

On aggravated autopilot, the remaining Punishers moved towards Diaz. Kagome shook her finger, warning them not to take another step.

"I said Take me in! That's an Order!" He roared. Kagome crouched down and nimbly spun the katana in her hand, telling the Punishers to stop without saying a word. A peal of sick laughter erupted out of her as they fought against the sure death embedded in following his order one way or another.

"DO it again!" she giggled at Diaz.
Blush-grinning over her bizarre pleasure, Diaz threw his head back. "Take me In! Now! It's your duty!!" He bellowed.

She sputtered with laughter as four of the Punishers charged straight into her slashing blade. Blood-thirst exploded in her chest as Kagome went wild. She downed mouthfuls of it as she cut through them like a butcher.

Diaz stepped out her way and took it all in, drenched in pride and their blood as she worked. Gore that hit him dried almost instantly and flaked off due to the fire that churned inside of him, creating a strange cloud of hazy red dust around him in the clearing as hunks of the four fell to the ground.

Upon contact with the stag's horn club moss coating the clearing, the chemical that coated the broken hulls of the exoskeletons still vice-gripped into chunks of felled Punishers went spasmodic. Kagome dove behind Diaz in the haze of red dust as the remains of the Punishers spontaneously combusted into black ash.

The blood-soaked Kagome roared in satisfaction and set her sights on the last remaining Punisher who'd ripped himself away from the slaughter and cowered in shock, traumatized by seeing the force of the Fugue firsthand. Panic yanked him up as her eyes caressed him in his hiding place and he ran for his life.

Diaz chuckled as she sprinted after him, screaming "It's too late!! Don't run now!" at the top of her lungs through the woods.

The Punisher screamed like a wild animal as he blindly fled into a devilish forest he'd been sent into many a times to kill senselessly, only to end up entangled in the dragnet of webs Kagome's hair had made through the trees. She yanked him down from her snare, dragged him back to the clearing where Diaz waited and threw the sniveling thing at his feet.

"I miss you, Bayh-" Diaz murmured dementedly. Kagome looked up in shock.

"Every aspect of your crazy ass-even this bizarre blood-lust part-" Diaz whispered affectionately.
"I miss you too-" She barked softly. "Every day of this so called Afterlife-"
"I Love you-You have to know that-"
"I know," Kagome said hoarsely, then shook the sentiment off.

"Things will be made right in the end- Do your- that glorious thing that made a Master Builder out of you- I'll take care of the little girl. I always do."

Kagome stepped away from him, wiped some of the glistening gore off her arm with a hand streaked with Punisher soot, raised two blood- drenched fingers up to her lips, pressed them to her mouth and tossed a bloody air-kiss at Vayo Kahn Diaz. It landed on his cheek as Kagome Arachne ran off into the woods towards water.

"Have fun with that thing-" she called out over her shoulder as the Leuce swallowed her from sight.

"Oh, I will-" Diaz growled.

chapter thirteen

The comfort child-prince of purification Hezuz ignored the admonition of the crone to not flinch when it first hit his senses.

He knew she had gotten perverse pleasure from every single one of his open reactions of disgust towards the atrocities she ordered upon any entities stupid enough to position themselves as martyrs against the Anannke's twisted protocols of purity.

The things Hezuz had seen since being unceremoniously installed and wordlessly accepted beside the Anannke as if he'd sprung from the pit of hell that roared from her belly would have broken the strongest in the realm if they'd had any semblance of heart left. For him, the carnage was nothing. It was her need to abuse that turned his stomach.

Her violence was of no import to him because he somehow knew there was not joy but despicable necessity compressed into every wretched call she made against the martyrs who had fought through hell to plead for justice before her. Even in his child-like, angry, half-lit state he intuited that her raging against them like a vindictive machine vindicated every martyred complainant that she wholesale slaughtered a second time.

Her need to dispose of them and the possibility of them receiving justice by any terms other than paths of purification ordained by her deposed the Anannke in the child Hezuz's eyes each and every time. The Anannke's awareness of the audacious nature of his disgust was what had led to the term of endearment she mockingly used to refer to him.

"Come on...*Heartless~*" the nickname seeped out of the corner of her mouth as she playfully poked at him telepathically.

Hezuz narrowed his eyes self-consciously.

The hand he'd aimed for his chin grazed the bizarre indentation in the center of his chest where his heart should have been.

It was a pigeon chest that made no sense seated in a seeming position of power in the midst of such vainglorious perfection . "Maybe that was why she left it." Hezuz had seethed repeatedly, "so the jab would cut all the more. Whatever- I don't need a heart to see she's a-"

He was instantly recaptured by the strange, childlike visions he'd found himself submerged in so often that he stopped trying to discern which was his true reality.

The fire throttling through the sky he felt strapped to melted into the flames and flashes of the incessant, pompous rites of purification rituals that lurched so restlessly towards blotting out all imperfections that might counter claims of purity that it made the eyes and teeth ache.

"I mean it this time..." The Anannke growled softly, her telepathy consciously piercing the only place in the complex he'd ever found to hide. "Do. Not. Flinch."

Erratic shadows flitted across the surface of the liquid gold floor. The heads of the nobles attending The Anannke and the boy Hezuz looked up as a murmur of confusion ricocheted across them.

chapter fourteen

Diaz grabbed the Punisher by the hair.

"You- and I- are about to go clean up the mess that I *know* you and your little hunting party made-" he snarled and tore back through the woods back towards the child's clearing, slamming the conjoined heads of the Punisher against every tree trunk he could along the way.

When they arrived, the carnivorous birds shot up into the air in a giant cloud. He looked around in horror. All that was left was bloody, broken bodies, gilded picture frames and weapons of war that glinted in the half-light of the Leuce, weaponry that had been of little use for the Punishers against the enraged dreams of the child's future self.

Diaz angrily threw the Punisher onto the pile of destroyed priceless art, blood and bones. He landed with a thud against the body of a Punisher whose compressed skulls still trapped in their cage had been picked clean by the birds and started to scream.

"Stay there!" Diaz ordered as he tossed bodies that had fallen on the outskirts of the battle and remnants of paintings on top of auto-piloted ANC that cursed under it all, struggling against the command, attempting to move but unable. Diaz blasted fire through his palms to burn up the blood soaked grass so there would be no draw to Punishers in the future. The flames crawled towards the center of the circle.

The base of the pyre of bodies and bones caught and exploded into an unquenchable spiritual fire like the one inside of Diaz that the Punishers had first been sent out to recapture.

He climbed the bonfire, the last color in him draining with every step towards the top.

He yanked the last Punisher up out of the detritus by the conjoined arm onto the top of the hill of fire with him.

"Get ready for the glory that comes with bringing me back-" Diaz snarled in the face of the two beings forcibly fused into one and punched the Punisher in the chest.

Everything exploded, shooting Vayo Kahn Diaz and the ANC2 up into the sky engulfed in flames, the clearing below now nothing more than a charred chunk of black in the midst of a dark forest.

chapter fifteen

The purified Nobles began to shriek as fires erupted inside their heads. Blood poured out of their ears due to the violent crack of thunder overhead. They cried out, looking for help from the Anannke who sat on the edge of the fray, indifferent. The eyes of the horrified nobles tore away from her and looked up towards the sky as the Anannke played with her hair.

Hezuz glowered at the Master of Fates as the tigers made their way out of the area, oblivious to this chaos being any different than the mayhem that erupted to entertain the Anannke or satisfy her appetites.

A flaming comet suddenly slammed into the glass domed eye above the center of the space. Nobles screamed as everything went flying, stampeding to corners of the room for shelter. All except a glowering Hezuz and Fate herself. The burning meteor quickly sunk halfway into the gold room. Its composition shifted from a ball of fire into a enormous, pulsing cluster of iron filaments that exploded in a whirling inferno of white heat, stabbing every screaming being that writhed in the corners with bolts of fire.

Nobles coated with the shards looked helplessly at one another as they began to morph into pillars of crumbling salt. Sure a Savior of some sort had finally arrived to set them free, the holy folk lined up in the floor howled with joy as giant drifts of worthless, dirty salt rushed down into the grates bolted over the trenches and filled their open,wailing mouths before they could think to shut them. They choked on the salt of the Earth their works had made useless, buried alive in the bowels of the purification sector of the Empyrean.

chapter sixteen

Anukai and Gabryl tore through underbrush and whitewashed aspen trees towards a ravine full of giant boulders.

"We're almost there-" Anukai whispered.
"Keep your head down!" Gabryl hissed nervously as they scampered down towards the first of the stones. "Wait- This doesn't look like where we started-" he swiveled around clumsily, alarmed by the changing landscape.

"We're really upstream- there's a spring up in the rocks that we have to get to up ahead," Anukai said breathlessly. "It's been dry for a while but I think it should be flowing by now. I know I still have people alongside it-"

"People? You mean like in the paintings?" he asked as he ducked to stay as close to the terrain as possible. His legs got tangled with hers and they fell out into the open with a thud.

"You'll see," she whispered after they both caught their breath for a bit. "Down by where the water opens- Let's go-"

They pulled each other up onto their feet and moved further into the gorge. The harsh, parched landscape dug into his eyes.

The boulders seemed to have broken due to impact the deeper they traveled, the place making his skin crawl after the Leuce's protective darkness. He felt exposed, vulnerable and wasn't able to erase the feeling that he somehow knew she did too, even as she led the charge. As they hit the bottom of the ravine, the trickle of water that had been hidden by the boulders began to crawl alongside them, and everything shifted to the color of bird droppings and dried mud.

Gabryl tried to stay focused on where they were going but

since he didn't know where he was the newness of everything called out to be taken in. Even worse, he felt watched.

He couldn't shake the sensation of eyes on the both of them. Gabryl glanced over his shoulder one more time and saw a long, dark shadow dart behind a rock. He stopped in his tracks.

"What in the hell was *that*?" He cursed so hoarsely that Anukai stopped and turned around.

Gabryl pointed to what looked like gigantic conical piles of sun- bleached shit topped with heaps of dried grass scattered along the tops of some of the larger boulders they'd just traveled through.

Anukai laughed. "Oh- that's where They live-"
"That's how *what* lives?" He asked, even more bewildered.
"Not what- whom~" Anukai blush-grinned.
"Who lives in that? That looks like Dragon crap-"
"How do you know what Dragon crap looks like?" She asked, grinning.

"Oh you think you're the only one who-" he started, indignant at what he rightfully took her smirk to mean. "Look- I may only be day-tripping here with you, but I got my own world too! And mines has dinosaurs And Dragons!See? There's a difference! Betcha didn't know that, did you? Real ones, not all these crazy killer monster metal, laser beam things like this place!" He yowled.

The fear he'd had to bottle up to escape what they'd run from sputtered out of his exhausted body. "If I didn't have my own thing I wouldn't even be able to play with you in the first place! And your place is crazy, by the way! You got me covered in mud, lost most of my clothes, and-" he fussed.

"No, no, no-" Anukai tried to calm him down as he glowered at her, angrily pulling his t shirt back over his head correctly. "I'm sorry, sheesh- I didn't mean it that way," she murmured, "I got people-" she continued. " A clan-My OWN Clan- that I made, better than the one I got stuck with back-" she paused and looked around.

" umm...it does look kind of creepy, huh?" Anukai tried to chuckle convincingly as it dawned on her he wasn't just angry. He was scared.

"They do kind of weird things...but I've learned you gotta let people do how they do and live how they want to live...Or they might get angry and try to eat you-" Anukai sighed.

Gabryl looked around warily."Eat me?!" he yelled.

"Come on- don't slow down," she sung out as she threaded her arm through his and pulled him forward. "Dragons and Dinosaurs? Whoa! The battles must be wild~"

"Yes, they are," he said curtly as he let himself be dragged.

chapter seventeen

The people of Anukai quietly crouched along the perimeter of the rocks.

They were not used to unannounced visits by the One who made them, and were all the more alarmed to see another alongside the One, and that they had been running.

Usually when the One came there was a wild celebration of the One to mark the sanctity of the One's sojourn among them.

But this time, the One had not even stopped.

The smell of war in the atmosphere made no sense. They had massacred all offending parties of their own tribe only moments ago in a past that spun backwards into forever.

Warily, the remnant of the clan went into warrior mode. Forty-five agile bodies coated themselves in oily black mud. They massaged it into the beautiful tendrils that danced in elaborate plaits and halos of hair unique to each head. The glistening black was even rubbed across shiny white teeth until their mouths became black abysses with bright red tongues that they wagged at one another, practicing muted yells of attack.

The electric whites of their eyes shot sparks as they blinked against the glare of the over-saturated sky that spun from a garish green up to a caustic red the highest up they could see. They became reflective shadows that moved across the bleached terrain.

Handfuls of them scampered up and over the edge in silent swan dives, quietly tumbling down between the boulders and out onto the river's edge at measured intervals.

Each one stood with hands in fists that rested on hips, stances of territorial aggression taught that would be seen with pride by the One that made them if only the One turned back.

The rest of the People of Anukai crawled along in the shadows above, blackened teeth bared, tongues silently wagging as they made their way.

chapter eighteen

The fiery filaments of the combusted comet made their way out of the dank salt the Nobles had transformed into, magnetized to the liquid gold that coated the floor.

The Anannke floated over towards the gleaming ground. The eyes of Hezuz followed her, oblivious to the nobles turned to salt all around him. The filaments slowly shifted out of her way in the shape of footprints as she glided a few inches above all of it.

Smirking, the Anannke trailed past him, bent down and lobbed his ornately carved sandals back to him without a word.

A gold crane with a belly full of writhing snakes spread out along the back of her undulating outyr as the fabric gently billowed in her wake as he watched.

The Anannke raised a brow, feeling the pressure of Hezuz's accusing stare as she languidly lifted her arm in front of her face and over her head as if removing a veil.

Suddenly the space became dark, dungeon-like. The eyes of Hezuz closed to recalibrate to the sudden change of atmospheric pressure.

chapter nineteen

"...What did you make them out of?" Gabryl asked after walking for a while in silence, less on edge the further they got away from the giant rocks.

Anukai shrugged. "Same stuff everybody makes them out of," she said simply and pointed to the cracked ground under their feet. He continued to walk at a slower pace than her to conserve his energy. She tried not to say anything about it.

"I just don't know how many are left- they kill each other off a lot, for reasons I don't really understand. But overall, they're Good. Hey-why are you moving so slow?"

"How can you call them good if they kill each other?" he asked philosophically.

"Just because they do something bad doesn't mean that they are bad." she whispered. "They still are mine. I still made them and I still love them. And they'll stop killing eventually, or they'll find a better reason to kill- or other at least things to kill instead of themselves."

She paused. "Or they'll wipe themselves out. I mean, I can always make more-and I always have more stuck somewhere ready to go just in case I have to, but I always forget where-" her voice trailed off, noticing Gabryl nervously look over his shoulder again.

Anukai grabbed his chin " They smell that...If you keep looking back in fear," she whispered through gritted teeth, "they're going to come for us...and tear *you* apart, not me-"

Gabryl yelped and took off running as Anukai cracked up. "*At least now he's moving faster*," she chuckled to herself.

"I was Kidding! Just Kidding!" she yelled out after him, laughing as she gave chase.

He scowled over his shoulder and ran even faster along the slowly widening river under the green into red sky.

Anukai got winded then pissed trailing behind him, not used to being outran. "You don't even know where you going!" she hollered after him.

"Yeah, but I know I'll get there first!" he yelled back over his shoulder cockily, a triumphant smile plastered across his face that made his eyes disappear under the apples of his cheeks.

Anukai's face darkened as she instinctively leaned down and scooped up a rock the size of a grapefruit, then a broken off, bent branch. Before she realized what she was doing she hurtled the rock at his head with her left hand and the branch a little past his feet with her right. He crumpled towards the ground as the branch connected with his feet just before the rock clocked him in his head.

Gleefully victorious, Anukai sped towards him.

The last thing Gabryl saw was Anukai as she frantically wiped at a torrent of blood that washed over his eyes as he blacked out.

She screamed hysterically, bewildered as he fell completely unconsciousness. Anukai grabbed him by the arms and dragged him onward as the consequences of hitting a very real boy in the head with a rock in a supposedly imaginary world spun out of control around her.

chapter twenty

Kagome did her best to erase every thought of Diaz from her mind as she slammed through the forest towards where the kids had run.

Her own hair webs evaporated from the trees as she crashed through them. The blood of the fallen Punishers had made her mouth thick, almost blotting out the memories churned by the taste of the realm, of the One she'd been in the Empyrean lifetimes ago.

"I can't think about it - it's done until it's done-" Kagome muttered to herself." I can't I can't I can't-I can't-" she rattled on.

Something made her pause as she neared the river.

The muscles in her neck bounced as her teeth set themselves on edge. The sky glistened off the rocks in the distance as if they were already soaked with blood.

Kagome waited with baited breath, then remembered nothing would register to send any beasts out from above until the cell she'd all but devoured was recognized as not coming back.

"I really Hope you got everything under control up there, Master Builder," was the last thought she allowed of the one called Vayo Kahn Diaz as she made her way under the cover of trees.

chapter twenty one

Hezuz reopened his eyes. The sky above was surely still red but he felt a lot farther away from it.

A swath of black, beaded material pushed the white strands of the Anannke's hair up off of her face like a giant tusk growing out of her head. The hair continued its ascent up towards a ceiling Hezuz could no longer see.

Her forehead was smeared with royal blue that melted into bright green across her brow, to a glistening red across the bridge of her nose and the apples of her cheeks. The gold dusted tones of her honeyed skin looked bronzed in the dark as the Anannke shifted suddenly.

A facet of her turned to look at him while what he'd been initially staring at froze. She laughed maniacally at him then quickly shifted back and reconnected with the rest of her as if nothing had happened. He blinked again, still rooted to the same spot as he watched The Anannke bend down.

The strapless, buttery black tooled leather gown she now wore gleamed in the dark as she took a finger full of the filaments on the still golden, wet floor and slowly dragged it along her eyes. Her orbs went from gleaming white like his to an abysmal black.

"Now let's see what... has been dragged in, shall we?" she Murmured, lazily slid her finger into her mouth and stepped back.

The filaments rose up in the air, burst into a cloud of ash for a split second then slammed into the floor with a loud crash, as if suddenly heavier than lead.

She smiled as some of her silver- white hair strung up above them dissolved into a shower of quicksilver.

Upon contact with the mercury, the ash morphed into the corpses of murdered Punishers and the charred paintings of what a little girl illegally trespassing in the Leuce intended to be someday anyway.

The Anannke studied the burnt paintings. She became angrier and angrier as she absorbed the intended outright insurrection against the story Necessity had scripted for the little one, captured balefully in full color and all but direct-mailed right to her due to a Punisher attack on her secret base that had somehow failed.

"This treachery will not be!" The Anannke snarled. "She will be the Abomination that I wove her up to be!" She cut her eyes towards the center of the refuse. A Punisher, barely alive, shivered next to the naked corpse of the one and only Ourgos of the Light-bringer class who'd been forcibly reconfigured into the Empyrean Master Builder Luc. Vayo Kahn Diaz at the behest of the spiritually petty members of the Tryage.

The Anannke glided over to the Punisher and grabbed it by the chin to stop its teeth from chattering. "Poor thing," she purred. "I can just imagine what he did to You -"

The black eyes of The Anannke flickered as a few strands of black hair tangled in the Punisher's exoskeleton glinted in the murky light of the space.

She sucked her teeth as the visage of the blood-soaked, long lost Kagome, once reared as the Anannke's offspring in preparation for the long awaited rescission of the Puryf throne flashed before her eyes for the first time in millennia as the ANC's last coherently lifted thought.

"I stand corrected." The Anannke seethed, "What *they*- what they did to you."

The Anannke dropped the Punisher back on the floor and slammed her foot down onto the release unit at the center of the exoskeleton that trapped the beings, unlatching them next to the corpse of Vayo Kahn Diaz.

The Androgyne disengaged and male and female rolled away from each other to die, exhausted but free, fingertips still dancing back towards the body of the other for comfort as they internally crossed over.

The Anannke grunted, grabbed the corpse of Diaz by the hair and began to drag him out of the room, "As for you, I will keep you here, twisted up in me, dead and alive, until you tell me exactly what *you* have to do with the absence of MY Kagome-"

She got all the way to the door before she became aware of Hezuz again. The corpse of Diaz hit the floor with a thud.

The Anannke smiled darkly at him and growled. "Wise of you to watch. It's the only thing that kept you in the afterlife, and the only reason you can even hear what is afoot. Remember that. No matter what-"

Hezuz refused to flinch.

"Now as for all that you see before you," she whispered, "I want *you* to get rid of it. *That* one will Never become any of it.

No matter what she thinks in spite of me. *I* get to decide what she becomes. And I already have. Burn it. Burn ALL of it."

The Anannke casually reached back down into Diaz's hair and Roughly dragged Vayo Kahn Diaz's corpse out of the dungeon.

chapter twenty two

Hezuz shrugged his shoulders like the bored tween he physically was.

He oddly enjoyed the first direct order he'd ever been given in the place of so many beings begging to be ordered around by him. He slowly brought the palms of his hands together in front of him. Flames from his own internal fire leapt out.

He absently directed them at the pile of paintings, then the two beings that had been one, watching as they were slowly incinerated.

The future selves of the little girl reanimated in front of his eyes and glared balefully at him as they slowly burned within the heat of his eternal flames.

By the time it was all turned to ash, he was fully grown and utterly in love with someone who would never be allowed to be, in the afterlife or otherwise. He instinctively fell to his knees, deranged by the futility of love slammed into him like shrapnel.

Hezuz lowered his head to the ground as if wounded and lapped at the ashes, swallowing mouthfuls as he searched himself for the words to express how they tasted.

"They taste...Beautiful-" he whispered insanely as a film encased him inside. A ring of darkness rose up along the outer edge of his irises as the little girl's sacred song he'd been ordered to snuff out cloaked within him.

chapter twenty three

Blood. Everywhere.

Anukai tried not to look at the gore seeping into the ground as she dragged Gabryl's heavy body towards the river.

*"Don't worry! He's not going to - But why is there so much blood?! Why did he turn around?!"*her mind raced.

Anukai pulled him into the first cluster of reeds that she saw along the riverbank, not even noticing the bodies she'd built up out of mud and forgotten about nearby. Tiny waves lapped at the crown of his head as she pressed her ear to his nose and felt no breath against the side of her face.

"Breathe!" Anukai screamed at the top of her lungs,beating on his chest. "You can't die here! Not in here!!!" She smacked an out cold Gabryl in the face angrily as the gash in his forehead slowly started to gum up.

"I didn't mean to- I - I didn't mean it-" she wailed, trying not to hyperventilate as she leaned over him, smearing tears and snot anxiously back into her hair.

Tiny bursts of air began to come from his mouth as it slackened gently. Sobbing hysterically, Anukai collapsed next to him. Relieved, she slapped angrily at his still unconscious form. Her mind began to turn in on itself.

"You ruin everything! Everything!" She muttered to herself crazily. "You finally- You finally found a friend to play with for real, and look what you did! You might've k-killed-" she hiccupped. "They're right! You're a fucking killer- a monster, no matter- They were-" her voice hitched.

The reverb of accusations of adults that she could normally

keep away from her in here made her feel like she had bitten down on aluminum foil as she choked on them, blacking out alongside Gabryl in the reeds.

chapter twenty four

The mother screamed for her mom as the sound of erratic breathing erupted near her ear again.

Sour breath rattled beside her. "She's dead."

The mother sobbed, struggling against whatever she'd been tied down with in her sleep.

"Dead," the hoarse voice whispered again. "Know why? Of course you do, you know why...you of all people know why she's dead, don't you? Admit it-"

"I SAID Admit it!" The harsh voice roared, slashing the forearm of the strung up mother open again. "You know why! You know Exactly why she's dead! It's Your fault! YOU killed her- You did it, not me- YOU- and that's matricide!"

"I didn't kill her!" The mother wept, but was cut off.

"Yes you did! Oh yea you did..." echoed around the mother. "You know why? Because you knew...you knew what was happening to me, and she did too...because you told her! You told her! And she protected you! Instead of stopping it, she let it keep going on and protected you! She-"

The accusing voice whirled around the mother. "She let it continue when she could've stopped it- she looked me in the face all that time, knowing- all those years when I was just a little kid- I was three when you decided to keep letting that happen to me-" the voice hitched.

"But...I'm not so little now, am I?" The voice laughed.

The table the mother was tied to shook as a barefoot seven year old jumped up on it. "Yeah...I'm still a kid, but I'm not little anymore, am I, Ma?" She sneered into her mother's bruised face.

"I'm...I'm a monster right? Almost as Big as you already, right?" The kid laughed as her body bloomed into that of a ten year old. " Bigger! A quarter of an inch taller- you and your stupid friends never let me forget! I...I ruin everything, right?" The child hissed as her frame shrunk back to that of a seven year old.

Acrid spittle scattered across the mother's face as she tried to look away with her good eye. "Looking just like you used to as a kid, right? Look at me," the child muttered impatiently.

" I said Look. At. Me! Look! Look-" She smacked the mother in her good eye and the last remaining light went out of it.

"Oh no~" the child laughed. "Nuh-uh, I already told you...not, not that easy, oh no~ Not for you! Not for any of you, but especially not you two-oh no~" the child sang as she stood up on the table.

"Get up." She muttered. "I said Wake up, wake the fuck up" she warbled melodically in the dark. "Wake up, I said!" She screamed, kicking at her blinded mother tied to the table, the child's feet filthy with the blood she'd ritualistically drained from her.

The child calmed herself and crouched down next to the mother's broken face. "Remember....remember when you used to beat me...for peeing in the bed after the attacks?" The kid laughed darkly. "Kids do that, ya know...pee the bed when they're getting molested. Yeah, you knew it. That's why you beat me. You didn't want anybody to put two and two together." The child cackled in her ear.

"You said I was...ruining the bed you bought with your hard-earned money...remember that? But I wasn't-"

The mother began to sob again.

"Nope, not at all, in fact...I was healing it- I learned that-It's- so funny how all this goes, Ma...because- Pee? Heals Everything! Yep! Specially skin..." the child leaned in closer.

"An-please-just-let me die-" The mother choked.

"Shut up and listen!" The kid sang. "Because I'm smart. But know how I know this one?" she leaned back in. "Ya momma. The dead because of you old lady ova there. She said~ she used pee pee to make all the bumps on your brother's face go away- and I looked it up one of those times I was hiding at the library to not come home...turn's out...she was right!" The child laughed darkly as she stood up and straddled her mother's face.

"Amazing the magic learned from you fucking witches." She growled, dancing around as she emptied her bladder all over her mother's prostrate form. Instantly the bruises and cuts across the mother began to heal. Even her sight came back as the kid cut her free.

The mother slid off the table she had once moved so she and her own mother could walk around as they lobbed curses at the defenseless child who now tortured her. She stumbled over to the skinned corpse of the complicit grandmother, gathered it in her arms and rocked back and forth, her back to her own offspring she'd tried to destroy out of jealousy.

"I'm sorry Ma...I'm sorry for-I should've killed it like the others before her when I found out they were girls- I'm Sorry I let her ruin...everything-" the mother whispered wretchedly.

"Hi Ma," the kid whispered gently behind her, pitying her.

The mother cried out deliriously at the sound of her daughter's voice.

"Cold?" The child murmured as she came up and draped the skin of her grandmother around her shivering mother in hell for warmth. The mother shuddered and yanked the flesh of her own mother around her, wishing she could just disappear in it.

"You killed her soon as you told her, knowing she'd let you get away with it." The little girl said simply. "So...she's dead. Matricide. It was you...that made all this...necessary. All of it. It's Your fault. Not mine."

The mother rocked back and forth in the darkened chamber.

"You gave them the okay," she whispered. "Remember? You told them how much you hated me... because of how much Daddy loved me when I got here. And they were just as spoiled as you." The kid looked away as a wave of fire crested in her chest. "I was barely three."

The mother silently sobbed, shaking her head no as her daughter continued. "You sanctioned what they did next... gave the okay for everything else that happened. Yeah Ma...I know about that too."

The little girl gently grabbed her broken mother by the chin and made her look her in the eye. "Every single one of your children got raped repeatedly because of you. Even your golden boy. One stopped talking for four years, Ma. Because of what you let happen to me. You were so stupid, actually believing a troll who'd eat one kid left on a bridge wouldn't eat the other two left with it- "

" They're mothers now, too...and- I'm...I get to kill them all."

"Every single one of them will be here because of you. Because you were the oldest and you Knew better." The girl whispered as she stroked her mother's hair. "And now... You ruined their families too. It's all your fault. Every single matricide I commit is due to you- and their blood is gonna keep you here longer than mine ever will because... somehow, I'm gonna find a way...to forgive you, Ma."

"You Ruined everything. Not me. Because you were jealous of a baby. And spoiled ...by her. And she let you do this to me."

The little girl looked down at her bloody hands and held them up in the dank chamber.

"... It was never my fault. None of it. Nothing these hands can do because of what you let happen to me was my fault. Ever. I know that now...so I don't hafta be here with yall no more." she muttered.

The little girl's hands began to glow in the dark as the cursed blood flaked off of them. She pulled them in front of her face and found her way to the locked door as her mother sobbed in the dark behind her.

Bright light shone around its edge and through its strange shaped keyhole as soft music played on the other side of it. She looked at her pinky finger, then back at the keyhole and pushed her finger into it. The door popped open and the little girl gingerly stepped into the whitest white she'd ever seen. She looked back at her mother cowering from the glaring light.

"Admit what you did so you can... Get up." Was the last thing she said to the mother rotting in the hell she and the grandmother had made for the little girl.

"He's gonna be okay-" echoed around her as the spirit of the little girl discombobulated in the light.

chapter twenty five

"...Get up."

Diaz willed himself to move in spite of pain that seared through his system. An arm he could not feel was tethered to a cold, glistening stone floor, as well as his opposing leg.

Torrents of liquid mercury violently slammed into his chest, beating years of afterlife off of him. The downpour stopped only to let him to catch his breath as droplets of quicksilver smacked against his third eye, trickled down the bruised, exquisite bones of his face and slid into his lush, gasping mouth, choked down one globule at a time until he had been systematically devalued.

"*UP*, I said! We're not done yet-" The Anannke murmured throatily as she crouched down and nuzzled against his swollen face in the dark.

"Come on-" The Anannke coaxed, "You're already dead... you only think it hurts! It's just...clarifying-" she purred.

Diaz's left eye groped up towards the ceiling coated with the Anannke's hair while his shattered right cornea tried to reconstitute itself in the wet heat that rose up out of him.

"Good! Much better-" The Anannke whispered. "That's the kind of fight I expect out of an Ourgos of the highest caliber like yourself... otherwise this just isn't as much fun. Fight it- fight back against the dissolution-" she leered. "Make it matter ...so I can enjoy it all the more when I kill off another layer left in you."

"Now tell me what you did to my daughter!!" She screeched. Kahn's head rolled back on his neck as he struggled to communicate.

The Anannke yanked her head up towards the ceiling in alarm.

She sniffed the dank air as Vayo Kahn Diaz gurgled in response to her. The smell of incense bloomed around her.

A surprise approach.

"Hold that thought- you weak, whitewashed, supposed Master Builder~" she sneered over the remnants of Diaz splayed across the floor.

She plastered a tepid smile across her face then shape-shifted into something more presentable as red, green and blue curtains of state nothing in the Per-a complex would look behind crashed down around him. The intensity of the colors dug into Diaz's good eye like the splinters of straw rammed underneath nails until sensory sedition stopped during Puryf, making him roughly cry out.

The Anannke whirled around. The amount of life-force left in his scream showcased she'd been toyed with.

"Liar-" she muttered and burst into shards of light, the truth of her spirit naked and unashamed for him to see for one split second before the reality of a prisoner named Vayo Kahn Diaz evaporated from her memory.

The smell of temple incense flooded the atmosphere as they got closer to the Puryf complex, undesired, uninvited and unannounced.

chapter twenty six

Music suddenly bloomed into the heavy atmosphere around the bodies of lil Anukai and Gabryl as she came to.

It was full of static, scratchy like an old piece of vinyl played in a grandmother's parlor. Anukai wiped at her wet cheeks and peered into his face again as the words softly lilted around her.

"I found a dream that I could speak to, a dream that I can call my own, I found a thrill to rest my cheek to, a thrill that I am never alone oh yeah...yeah and you smiled you smiled oh and then the spell was cast, and here we are in heaven, for you are mine...at last..."

She leaned in closer and realized with shock that the music was coming out of the hole she'd put in his head with the rock. She started to laugh uncontrollably and cry at the same time. She looked around and saw some of her unanimated clan of clay men right there with them in the reeds for the first time as bloody water lapped towards them.

Gabryl started to snore softly. Anukai sighed with relief.

From the strange sound of things he was going to be okay. Shyly, she watched him sleep for a while.

She stuck her favorite thumb into his mouth whenever he stirred before she finally just gingerly laid her head down on his stomach. The song grated the atmosphere around them on a loop. It lulled her to sleep against him, her free thumb stuck absently into her own mouth.

chapter twenty seven

White light exploded as the rock connected with his forehead. Then everything went black.

Gabryl nervously raised his fingers to his forehead in confusion as wetness washed over him in the dark.

"Not again! Not here- Please-Please!!" he wailed.

His breath hitched in his chest as Gabryl cagily looked anywhere but down, knowing it was coming before he was ripped off the ground up into the air as a hail of fire popped like cherry bombs around him.

He spun violently in the air, the huge barrel of the discharging gun still smoking behind him as his feet tangled in covers he couldn't see, tripping him.

He plummeted roughly to the ground, the concrete he slammed into morphing into a blue and green splotchy carpet that shifted around him ethereally, like his impact had turned it to water.

He fought against the blackout as the face of an obviously terrified yet concerned, angelic little girl floated up into his consciousness, screaming at him to run and hide before it was too late as malignant voices inside his head screeched.

"Don't look DOWN!!" They cackled, strung up around his senses. They sung out like a Greek chorus as he took off.

But it was too late.

Gabryl saw light glowing under his chin and looked down as he ran. The holes ripped in his chest gleamed right before blood flooded out.

He screamed, crashing into and through mirror after mirror

until he collapsed and slid down a brick wall onto the ground.

"Not- not here- Please ! Not again! Don't leave me here to be- I can't- I can't I can't Do any- Help!" He stammered.

The numbness of the night terror that always came on the end of a bout of sleepwalking set in as the girl he always saw here stumbled past, trying to find a place to hide.

"I can't help her! Don't- don't make me watch again- there's nothing I can Do! I don't know what to do!" He cried out, trapped in his nightmare as the monster on the girl's heels scurried after its prey in the dark, unaware of Gabryl's paralyzed presence nearby as the beast pounced on its target.

"Dont look down!" The ghastly voices sang inside his head, intent on driving him insane all over again.

"Breathe!" The little angel from before screamed as her face broke through the static gathering in the nightmare like a pirate broadcast. "You- Can't Die- Trust-"

The word trust echoed around him as disjointed memories of the little Angel and Anukai's tears turning his chest to water swaddled him, pulling him up from under the weight of the nightmare that had tortured him every chance it got. The ghastly voices of his tormentors shook with panic as the dream shuddered, splintering around Gabryl in the dark.

"Show me…Trust…won't hurt you anymore~" Anukai's voice stuttered defiantly against his wet cheek in the dark alley.

Gabryl struggled up onto his elbows and, face wet, dejectedly looked down at his blood soaked chest then screamed so ferociously that everything around him froze.

He roared as his soul violently pushed the eight bullets that had slammed into him back out, each still hot bullet ripping open fresh skin as they rolled down his chest and fell to the ground. He collapsed back onto the concrete, a huge bloody hole with eight legs at the center of his sternum gushing as he roared in pain at the top of his lungs.

The nearby monster lunged over to Gabryl's torn open, screeching body, screaming at him.

"Sshut up! Sstop it! Sstop- Oh my Gahgah-" the demon riding the psychotic man hissed frantically.

The howling, bloody mess of Gabryl's little body pulled the man the monster was navigating back up to the surface and he retched before shooting out of the alley, leaving the girl he'd attacked and Gabryl barely alive as the little boy continued to scream.

chapter twenty eight

As she made her way towards the Tryage gate the Anannke breezed through terraces full of spiritual babies dressed in uniforms of red, green and blue clustered around the stoic beings clothed in white-washed burlap that led them in their rituals of re-education.

Bells chimed in the air as the beautiful bodies of jeweled Elohs- in-preparation playfully darted past the Anannke, boomeranging into place behind her, barefoot, tossing all manner of flower petals towards her feet as they traversed golden floors beneath cedar and teak beams.

Strands of gold unhinged from their necks and snaked through the air towards hers as her silvery hair spun into the softest white tendrils before darkening of their own accord to cottony black and red dreadlocks that hung behind her to the middle of her thighs.

Banners the color of bloodstains wafted down from rafters and twisted themselves around her naked hips. The scent of bruised rose petals filled the atmosphere with every step that The Anannke would have taken if she'd not floated, crushed by the weight of her presence in lieu of actual contact.

The Elohs in basic training giggled as the odor of roses fought against the scent of temple incense in the final courtyard they headed towards, a battle waged ahead of time in order to win the war.

The cluster of thirteen bejeweled, topless women paused behind the final curtain of state dyed the color of a night sky long since erased from their memories, the last membrane that stood between them and the heavenly outer Empyrean realm.

The Anannke was as indistinguishable among the Elohs to them as she was to herself in this state.

The thirteen ladies dropped to their knees and bowed their heads submissively as the final curtain of state parted.

Copper incense balls spun overhead on chains as the Tryage and all attending them in their three chrome-and- copper chaises came into opulent view.

On the other side of the technically always open gate, three different kinds of spiritual strength clustered around their grandest champions within the Empyrean realm as the Councilors reclined lasciviously.

The perfected sighs and resonating laughter of the cluster of 13 Elohs danced out into the courtyard that separated them.

chapter twenty nine

Sirens blared as paramedics loaded both the teenaged girl and bloodied little boy onto stretchers and rammed them onto the ambulance.

The little sleepwalking boy and the first to escape the serial killer who'd been slaughtering black girls across the tri-state area for ages sans any real pushback from the authorities bounced up and down in the ambulance as it slammed through traffic. Their almost lifeless fingers twitched against each other in the tight confines of the truck as the EMTs did their best to keep them alive.

"Any identification on either of them?"
"Negative- Hold on, lil guy! We're almost there!" The lead EMT whispered. "You're both going to be okay- you're both going to make it-"

Bright light exploded again as they were ripped apart, slammed onto gurneys and down different hallways in the hospital, the young woman to ICU, Gabryl to the pediatric intensive care unit.

Everything went to black again as Gabryl came in and out of consciousness.

"She's going to be okay- what about him?"
"He's going to have a bad scar, and they didn't find the bullets

that did this at the scene of the crime...but he's...I think he's going to be okay." The nurse whispered.

"Well, I hope so. That little boy's screaming saved her life-" another nurse murmured. 'Another minute with that monster and they would've found this little boy next to victim 73."

"Maybe now...the cops will do something to stop this sonofa-"

The doctor came in and nodded to his nurses before he leaned over Gabryl to check his vitals.

"I hope you can hear me, lil man," the Doctor whispered. "You're a Hero, you hear me? A Hero- You...you saved your friend's life with those lungs, you hear me? Screamed like Sonni Ali...roared like Shaka, like Hannibal himself... like a true African Warrior King-"

The doctor looked up at his nurses, then back at the broken little boy bandaged in the bed beside him.

"28 calls to 911 happened because of you tonight. Twenty Eight. Across a ten-block radius, in an area ambulances usually act like doesn't even exist. Your voice rang out like a prophet on a mountain, kid- Don't worry. Rest...we'll get you all the way back."

The Doctor kissed Gabryl gently on the forehead as the morphine he deftly administered reached its fingers up and took Gabryl back under.

"He was obviously sleepwalking. They're going door to door in the neighborhood now, trying to find both their families. He's gonna be okay." The doctor murmured as he stroked Gabryl's cheek.

Soft white light seeped in as the doctor's voice echoed around him the deeper he fell back into sleep.

chapter thirty

Gabryl's eyes popped open as the needle scraped roughly against the album playing in his head.

"What the-" he choked as he tried to sit up but caught sight of the corpse-like clay figures he was alongside and stopped short, staring at their slack-mouthed faces hesitantly until he was sure they weren't going to move.

He then felt the weight of Anukai's head on his stomach followed by a jolt of pain in his forehead where she'd whacked him with the rock.

The last of his honey-toned irises dissolved in a white-hot rage as he bit down on her thumb so roughly that he drew blood. Anukai screamed awake and curled up into a ball as he jumped on her and hit at every bit of her that he could, residuals of her beating on his chest cut by his subconscious with the crunch of the stick into his bowed legs and the arc of the rock in the air as it sailed towards him too quickly for him to veer out of its way.

Anukai tried to get away but he kept dragging her back. A new song began to erupt out of the hole in his head as he swung ferociously at her.

"Stop!! Ow!!I didn't- STOp!" She suddenly yowled up at him from fetal position, so loudly that he actually paused.

Anukai hesitantly peeked up and gasped because his eyes were glowing white in a way they weren't supposed to be able to do since he was real. "Your eyes-" she hissed in shock.

He glowered at her, "What?!- My eyes?! You hit me in the-" He began to kick at her again.

"I told you to Stop!! That's it-" She shrieked.

Anukai grabbed him by the ankles, yanked him down into the dirt with her and roughly knocked him into the river. She leapt on top of him and smacked at him as he hit back at her, both of them screaming at the other to stop as they rolled around in the shallows. Gabryl got up and sat on her chest, howling with wicked laughter while she cried out at the water that went up her nose.

"Oh yeah! You can't swim, can you?! Stop scratching me! Stop Scratching me- Stop it-" Gabryl hissed hysterically and dunked her head again and again.

On the third dunk Anukai's eyes flipped to pure white fury. She came up swinging and sunk her teeth into the first flesh that she made contact with. Gabryl screamed like he had been shot and tried to stagger away, but Anukai tackled him and maniacally wrapped her little fingers around his neck and pressed down as hard as she could. He swung out at her blindly, bruising her arms as she continued to strangle him with all her might. Something inside of Anukai snapped and she rambled repetitively, lost somewhere within her own rage as she tried to choke the life out of the little boy she'd just freaked out over having possibly killed moments earlier.

"-I told you! I told you but you wouldn't listen-" she snarled wildly. Gabryl violently swung and kicked at her but she wouldn't let go. She couldn't even hear him anymore.

"Anukai- Sto-p-p!!" He gasped as he tried his best to writhe away from her. Her head hung over him twisted into a scowl of wrath too big for her little face. As the last of the blood and oxygen began to drain from his brain, Gabryl opened his eyes one last time and locked eyes with hers.

They looked at each other in confused shock. Anukai released her grip on his neck, utterly stunned.

"Stop!!" Gabryl screamed as he brutally hit her in the mouth. She went flying over the half-hidden clay bodies of her clan and crashed down on the far side of them, parallel arcs of blood, spit and tears following in her wake and splattering across the clay face of one of her people.

The man of Anukai came to life with a start as the blood, spit and salt seeped into the clay and morphed it into skin as he animated. He found his maker crying softly as she wiped at her nose and split lip deep in the reeds, obviously hurt.

He bent down and clumsily wiped at her hair to get her attention, then smiled like a newborn at her due to just being awakened. She looked up at him listlessly as he took her chin. On contact he was embedded with the residuals from the battle that had just gone down.

The man of Anukai whirled around and saw Gabryl as the bruised and scratched little boy crawled inland, trying to catch his breath before he gave up and collapsed in a heap on the shore.

The man of Anukai spun back towards his maker and narrowed his eyes. He dropped her chin and started to lumber towards an oblivious Gabryl. Clay continued to turn to sinews up the back of the legs of the man of Anukai with each heavy step he took.

"No!- No-" Anukai hoarsely called out as she stumbled behind him as he went for the beat up little boy.

chapter thirty one

The chrome carriages sat like matryoshkas in a half circle on the hallowed, harsh terrain that surrounded the purification complex.

The heavy sedans levitated slightly, the magnetic field embedded into the ground unable to bear the hidden sins of those that they carried. Red ties that held the white ceremonial drapes along the cars were undone and raw silk unfurled dreamily out into the charged atmosphere.

The most Spartan of the carriages contained the First Head of the Tryage, known throughout eternity for the harshness of his ivory tower decrees towards those below as well as the totalitarian ways and means he used to ensure that the unspoken caste delineations he designed to cage humanity would remain forever in play in his highest quadrant of hell. His chrome- plated cage of light hovered the highest off the ground and he mistook it as a badge of celestial honor, brandished as universal proof that his path was the highest.

To First Head, everything was Old Guard, Black or White, and it showed in the way he'd handpicked his retinue. It was full of beings that in previous lives below were brawny Alpha men that bristled with perfection and thuggish Beta control freaks that happily lived out their version of heaven serving one that knew how to tell a man who knew not to ask questions what to do. They basked in the light of their highest high leading them to and fro like the empty shells engineered for intimidation that they were.

In the middle of the road drifted the chrome carriage of the Second Head of the Tryage, a being known to pride himself on his ability to make any spirit compromise, which was always the first step towards utter dominion over it.

Second took a seemingly more democratic, fake-liberal approach to all things brought to his attention. He was the Masthead of and for the people, as long as the people were too lazy to decide anything for themselves. His carriage was so baroque that those who danced in his altruistic eminence said it was adorned ironically, opposing the rhetoric on proletariat power unifying all causes that flowed so eloquently from his lips whenever his way was called on to feign taking the lead.

Second's entourage was filled with the best of the best, seen as the new Empyrean guard, truly spectacular citizens of the Highest High: A third had spent lifetimes throwing peace signs up in the air at protests and beating the daylights out of the sycophantic women who cleaved to them in the dark waiting to siphon off their always impending glory; A third were shape-shifters who'd repeatedly latched onto big-tickets based on how cool they looked in the uniform of this and that cause and whether or not they could get proof that they were *there, man,* right in the thick of it. They were oblivious to the fact that by standing for so many things so intensely for so long they'd crash and burn right into the cubicles of the establishment they'd been fake-rallying against, sodomizing themselves with file after file as they worked for peons that had purchased them like the highly priced pigs they'd always been under the surface;

Group three were the poster children for the rainbow coalition, smiling for all to see as they tried to block out the sound of whirlwinds eating away at them inside. They were imposters who'd spent life after life building up interethnic menageries to prove how post racial and liberal their narrow-minded asses were, hurtling to where the *action* was. They had also spent lifetimes destroying any that saw through them and had no desire whatsoever to be in awe of him. Within the new guard, the Beautiful ones were the most violent of all, taking any opportunity to get lost in the malignancy of the kill for the cause. Even with complete Purification and pompous self-flagellation bragged about every step of the way their putrefaction could never be erased.

And then there was Third.
The Third Head of the Tryage was slandered as Inexplicable.

When discussed at all in the realm it was pejoratively. The power of her rag-tag crew of pierced, tattooed, lascivious-looking, ambi-sexual hooligans in a fiery abode viciously devoid of touch was offensive and incomprehensible to the studied tastes of First and Second Head and all those who worshipped along their two roads in the Empyrean.

Third was the champion of those disparaged as Denizens within the realm, occupants within heaven the Citizens murmured must have gotten into the ever after through a loophole too coated with club-land lube and filth to be bothered with.

The Denizens surrounding Third were the only supernatural beings present at the gate who realized that they were free, with no need to take orders from the kind of beings they had already out-witted below. All others present were on sycophantic auto-pilot.

Third's faction was the only one that knew they were at the Puryf gate to grab at least one of their own before First and Second could get their hands on him again, and that there was nothing that anyone could do to thwart that intent.

The bearers of the spinning decanters of frankincense pumped their arms harder as the three units moved into position.

chapter thirty two

Gabryl whipped around and looked up into the enraged face of The Man of Anukai in horror as he raised his muscular, still partially terra-cotta arm to strike him. Anukai sandwiched herself between the two of them. "No-" she whispered hoarsely.

"...We were fighting, because I-I hit him in the head- cause he tried to get away- I - I just didn't want him to leave- but I almost killed him trying to make him stay with me-but he almost died." She sobbed.

The man of Anukai narrowed his all-white eyes and wagged his tongue at Gabryl in a mute war cry. No words came out but Gabryl understood clear as day that the thing was designed to rip him apart for much less. The new man of Anukai pointed an obscenely long finger at Gabryl and twitched it quickly from side to side and raised a sharp brow.

"I'm sorry too!" Gabryl yelped. "I don't know what happened but I- I'll never..." his voice wilted.

The man of Anukai nodded when he saw that Gabryl knew never to hurt her again. The new man shrugged his shoulders, shook his head at the little girl sheepishly, then walked towards the river to baptize himself. Anukai and Gabryl looked at each other for a long time and then back out at the brick colored man as he cleaned himself in the river.

"So...that's one of your-" Gabryl whispered.
"Yeah-" She mumbled. "I'm sorry-" she whispered quickly.

"Me too- I'm sorry too." He growled, absently massaging his throat.

They awkwardly hugged each other, sat down and looked out over the river.

"You got good aim." He croaked as he inspected her scratches on his arms. "And my voice is probably going to sound crazy for the rest of my life," he muttered.

"Yeah, well look what you did to my hair-" She grumbled and pointed to the wild mess atop her head. "And I got bruises- You fought me like I was a boy-" she whispered, honored.

"-You-You tried to kill me-" he muttered back, astonished. They sat in silence for a while longer.

"I don't think we should fight again-no matter what-We- we could kill each other-" she whispered. "We have to make a pact never to-"

"No matter what-" Gabryl whispered in agreement. They looked at all the bruises, scratches and blood on them. "We look like...barbarians," Gabryl started.

"Well-" she whispered "That we can fix that- come on!"

They jumped up and headed to the river and began to coat each other's bruises and scrapes with wet clay. Anukai pressed a sliver of it onto the cut on his forehead and gingerly kneaded it in with her fingers. She made a small dent in the center of his forehead for her thumb to rest in like she did with the rest of her clan, like he was one of hers. He pinched and prodded at the mud he'd placed on her split lips until they stuck out as if double-stuffed. They splashed into the water they'd just been trying to kill each other in and played happily in its shallows as the man of Anukai crawled to sun himself on shore, fully skinned and sanctified.

chapter thirty three

The mob of mothers watched the two morsels playfully wrestling in the waves from the far side of the riverbank.

The last time they'd feasted on anything more than the damp yet desiccated husks of kingdom sacrifices that had floated downstream into their tributaries felt so long ago that the memories were like the dust that danced in their crusty eyelashes that they angrily scratched at. Fallow reverberations of former tastes rattled across the surfaces of their forked tongues as they coughed hoarsely against the famine.

Faint moans of cannibalistic hunger ebbed and flowed through them, lost in the rush of water down river and the rustle of wind through the reeds that kept their bent, ravenous bodies hidden from sight.

Blind, they held matted heads of hair in their gnarled hands, licking parched lips until the warm pulsing joy of the sound of children playing slid them over to the edge of the riverbank.

They slithered onto the surface of the churning waters and sunk into the river that was clogged on their side by silvery, hairlike seaweed.

Using echolocation between riptides in the water they stealthily plotted their slow and steady course back towards the side of the river that sustained the only life force that satiated their lost souls, the flesh of their once most favored prey.

chapter thirty four

Peals of laughter spurted out of Anukai as Gabryl helped her find her weightlessness of the water and she began to float with confidence.

They bobbed above and below the surface of the river as their skins healed, the sensation of joint recalibration tickling like sea grass that danced across the tips of their toes underwater.

"Don't be scared," Gabryl whispered as they took turns sitting down so that the waves lapped at their ears and their feet floated up towards the surface. "I won't let you drown, I promise- you just have to get used to it-"

Their joy wove their spirits together even tighter. All memories of the anxiety, terror and rage evaporated as they opened and closed their eyes against the soft pressure of the water.

"You sound like Kermit." Anukai giggled out of nowhere as she relaxed and gingerly tried to let the toes of one foot float up

towards the surface with the other securely planted in the riverbed, holding onto him for dear life.

"What?Like Kermit? Kermit talks through his nose! I don't sound like that!" Gabryl laughed at the craziness that came out of her even before she said it like he could hear her giggling over it ahead of time.

"Like a crazy frog. But I like it!" She howled like a coyote when he splashed her, tickled with her twisted view of him as much as she was by picturing him as a fighting frog. "That's why you can swim! Cause- You're amphibian-ish! Able to live in two whole worlds! Tadpoley- Imma call you Taddy! Can I call you Taddy?! Will you answer to it as long as nobody else knew why? I won't tell nobody why I call you it, I-Promise!" Anukai sang.

Giddy, she rambled on, high off what she'd always known recalibration would have to feel like, even though this was her first taste of it. Gabryl kept trying to look at her the way adults try not to be caught up in the silliness of their children in public, but he couldn't because she was having too much fun. He whirlpooled.

"Nut-" He muttered happily as he let his body relax into the weightlessness of both the water and her playing with him.

"Taddy! *Vivre le resistance*!!!!" she cried happily with a thick French accent as she splashed back, drunk off the joy in the air.

"You are making no sense-" he cackled, pausing as he reached over and caught her eye so she wouldn't be surprised as he dunked her, still holding onto her with one hand, basking in the first nickname he'd ever gotten from another kid and liked, as close to smitten as a boy could be before boys saw girls as girls.

They held hands and their breaths under the surface and grinned at each other, air bubbles dancing the sincerest thoughts children could have between them.

chapter thirty five

The two Punishers crept in the shadows along the riverbank, their arrival drowned out by the sound of the kids at play who'd floated farther out into the water.

"There's more than the- but there's two to four of us- And what of the rest?"

The exoskeleton-corralled Nefilim looked down at the copper rings that normally spun on their fingers synchronizing them to the rest of their entourage. As they held their hands towards each other, the rings shifted but as they moved them out towards the Leuce the rings were motionless.

"Maybe they've taken him in? Doesn't matter- we must Act-" The exoskeleton of one of the Punishers started to stand before he did.

"But-" The ANC2 still crouched in the underbrush stiffened as the two spirits trapped in the house of him fought against what they were called to do next by protocol.

"They weren't the assignment- and if the others have taken the Fire-starter in- technically we don't even have to be here anymore-" The exoskeleton danced along the perimeter of its skin and pressed meanly into its flesh as the other Punisher bent back down.

"What are you trying to say?" It whispered to its comrade as it watched the two in one beside it suddenly start to struggle against the metallic cage clamped down onto it.

"They're just kids- they're just kids-I don't want to do

this anymore- we can't-" The male and female housed within the distressed ANC2 pulled away from each other.

Their faces disengaged from the eternal kiss that fused them into one and two heads and four arms unwound as they attempted to pry off the thing that trapped them together.

"I'm tired of killing children for this–protocol- we can't do this any-"

The other Punisher looked away until its comrade stopped squirming and sunk back down into its cage of capture.

"It is our dutiful service for having been spared-" it whispered woodenly.

"They shouldn't even be here- the faster we-finish this-" It slammed its fist into its palm, *"the faster we can despoil from all of- remove the residuals in Puryf-"*

The Punishers sighed collectively at their assigned fate.

chapter thirty six

The man of Anukai yawned against the sky overhead, completely unaware of the Punishers slowly materializing beside his crown and chest. They were upon him instantly.

The man of Anukai was muffled by two of the hands as he tried to scream. One Punisher held down his head as its partner began systematically cracking newly formed bones in arms and legs into shards. Rivulets of blood and baptismal waters poured out of the man as the dry heat of the blows drove his wetness out into the clay and sandy loam.

The Punishers rose up and slammed down simultaneously into the clay man's second and third chakras. He exploded into flames on the beach like a bonfire.

chapter thirty seven

The children came up for air and smelled smoke. They looked back at the beach in confusion and saw the four arms of each of the two Punishers fuse back together as they rose up and started towards them with determination.

Anukai screamed, fighting against Gabryl as he looped his arm around her waist to pull her farther out into the water. Her screams splintered in Gabryl's sensitive ears and he faltered in the waves. Anukai slipped slightly from his grasp, panicked and began to kick furiously in every direction, forgetting how to float all over again as she sunk in the river, swallowing water with every scream she couldn't stop.

The atmosphere changed as the cannibalistic mothers that were lurking towards the two children underwater looked up in alarm at the sound of terrifyingly familiar cries. En masse they fled back to their shore, crashed through the reeds up into fields of corn and ran from a howl every cell in their post life body remembered from some other slice of eternity.

Gabryl fought against the pain in his ears and her limbs as they flailed out. "Stop it! I promised you I wouldn't let you drown!" He whispered roughly against the side of her face.

Gabryl yanked the rest of her towards him, wrapped himself around her and did the only thing he could think to do. He swam back towards the shore as the Punishers got closer to it. Anukai couldn't even scream anymore. The water in her nose and lungs hurt like nothing she'd ever felt before as she began to black out.

chapter thirty eight

Out of the trees charged the black shiny shadows of the rest of the people of Anukai. They swarmed the Punishers, practiced rebel yells finally erupting out of their chests.

The Punishers looked back in alarm right as the first of the people of Anukai blitzed them. The fire-throwing beasts of burden slashed at them in a cloud of dust and sent sprays of bright blood across their kindred. The dirt created a bloody film of protection across the skins of the remaining people of Anukai that made them invincible. The Punishers threw flames at the oily bodies of the people of Anukai as they continued to charge relentlessly.

That fire transfigured across the top of them as the People of Anukai fought even harder, literally aflame. They passed the flames amongst themselves until every member of the clan was on fire, then attacked the Punishers again, attempting to rip the twos apart into the four they'd revealed themselves to be. The women of Anukai brutally tackled the Punishers to the ground as the men did to them what they'd just seen them do to one of their tribe from the trees, the first time an outsider had attacked one of their own.

One of the women of the clan instinctively slammed against the center of the exoskeleton unit that housed the two in one and they uncoiled from one another in a panic. The people of Anukai hissed and collectively stepped back, still lit on fire as the two freed ANC2s looked up at them in shock.

"Run!" the freed two screamed in unison then froze, startled at the sound of their own voices outside of their heads for the first time in forever. They jumped up, slammed through the rank of the still-shocked people and took off for the water's edge.

chapter thirty nine

Gabryl pulled Anukai up onto the shore and tried to push the water out of her unsuccessfully, not even seeing the two freed beings running towards them.

The bruised and burnt freed man and woman stopped short as Gabryl looked up helplessly, tears running down his face, too afraid for Anukai to fear the two beings that loomed over them. The people of Anukai roared as they moved towards the Punisher who had not yet gotten away.

"*...Roll her onto her side,*" the freed woman whispered softly to the little boy as she looked over her shoulder towards her mate, battle cries raging behind them. "*-do this.*"

The woman looped her arms around her mate, grasped her fists in front of him and pressed back towards herself. Gabryl nervously copied her, curled around Anukai on the damp shore.

Anukai came to and quickly began to spit up water, bewildered by hearing the roar of her people firsthand for the first time. She looked around cagily, then up into the face of the freed woman, surprised.

The Nefilim blinked, nodding as communion passed between the two in streams of consciousness neither would have been able to explain. Anukai acquiesced to a silent request as Gabryl closed his eyes and held onto her even tighter, too exhausted to be afraid of anything anymore.

The man and woman dove into the water and disappeared under the waves.

The People of Anukai spun around en masse and saw the soles of the freed couple's feet as they sunk, the two children breathing heavily on the beach. The people of Anukai moved towards them as a unit but Anukai held up her hand to stop them.

The still fused Punisher saw his chance for escape and ran towards the woods with all his might. Straight into the tip of a katana as Kagome stepped out of the shadows.

chapter forty

Defensively, the Punisher swung out its curved blade and slashed the underbelly of Kagome. Her sick smile of enjoyment didn't budge. The sight of her indifference and the strange blood that seeped out of her made the Punisher slowly step back out into the open as she advanced.

The people of Anukai retreated as the long haired one they'd learned to kill from in the dark came out into the light. "She" was well known, respected and feared by them after observing her Punisher hunts through the Leuce from the shadows of One's Sanctuary.

"Nice trick you have there, splitting apart like that-" Kagome purred, sounding just like The Fate she had erased from her memory. She contemplated the new intel, ignoring the trickle of blood that danced above her belly button.

"Was never told that... Above...but it explains why I've always felt so full after, does it not?" She growled. "Come now.. .Honor and Obey me-Sit –sit-sit-" Kagome whispered absently as she motioned the Punisher to the ground with the bearing of a Siamese monarch.

It sunk down heavily into the still burning gore of the man of Anukai it had just helped to decimate.

The people of Anukai knelt down behind him in honor of their fallen newborn son.

"Good-good-good...Now should I *Finish Him*- I mean It?" Kagome growled as if questioning herself aloud, "Or allow it to Finish Itself?" she whispered as she slammed the katana into the torso of the Punisher and cleanly out through the other side before she even finished the question.

She brought the blade back through in the opposite direction to end where she had begun. The Punisher fell back as sacred blood from both it and Kagome's wound went up in the air due to the brutally exquisite force of her movement. Her blood gleamed, full of brimstone against the blood of ANC_2s that glinted like crushed rubies as it sprayed across the faces of the people of Anukai and the forms in the nearest reeds.

Newly born clay clansmen crawled out chuckling as if let in on a new joke and lined up with the rest of the People of Anukai as the splice of blood soaked into the bank. Kagome peered down at at the still fused yet dying Punisher.

" I watched your kind throw away so many small bodies like garbage an eternity ago-" she murmured and gently pressed the latch at the center of the unit she'd always thought was just for decoration.

"And all this time, you were just...nothing more than slaves."

The male and female took their last breaths together then unhinged from one another.

Hands held, they died.

chapter forty one

Hezuz could hear each step of his attending Elohs as their dainty feet slapped against the floor behind him in a cloud of rose and saffron. The falsely procured affection that had irked him as a coddled spirit-child enraged him as a full-blown being and the Elohs had long since learned in eternity not to cross him, staying a million miles away internally instead.

He smirked to himself, feeling them collectively hesitate as he slowed then sped up again. The bejeweled horde of temple priestesses lurched after him, knowing that any invasion of his space could end in fire.

Suddenly, over the delicate din of the insanely pretty, nervous women he heard a harsh gasp. He elegantly raised his hand in the air. The gaggle of Elohs that trailed behind him froze and sensed that he was beyond displeased. Beautifully textured heads hung as they backed away from him before he could blow. They shuffled for cover without daring to catch any eye around them for fear of being openly accused of treason due to it down the line.

Hezuz turned his head slowly so as not to disturb anything in the atmosphere that might have the capacity to pick up the fact that he was sensing something he should not. Heavy curtains of state hung across a hallway he knew to be normally unblocked. As the rose petals the Elohs had tossed rolled along the floor around him he smelled something he couldn't place. Whatever was behind the curtains of state was not part of the head of this particular house the way all else claimed and clamored to be. He ripped the curtains open.

In a puddle of quicksilver and chained to the floor was hunched a stricken and starved albino adolescent, a boy with a shock of

Afro textured platinum blond hair stuck to his head like a rooster bloodied in a cock-fight.

Hezuz peered into the face of the teenager. His mind raced to place the features, bone structure, anything that would explain the instant, severe kinship with him that exploded in Hezuz's heart.

Anannke dragging the corpse of a much older version of him through the bowels of the citadel an eternity ago flashed before his eyes. Mindlessly, he slammed the heel of his foot into the chain that held the being who had literally had years of life tortured out of him.

Diaz gasped as his eyes ripped open. The filmy membrane of rebirth still plastered to him, he began to dry-heave chrome-colored liquid out of himself, which morphed into reflective shards and magnetized up, slashing through the air to embed themselves along the meridian lines temporarily visible across his still lucent skin. His body rocked as if hit by electricity.

Hezuz hoisted Diaz up over his shoulder as the boy struggled against being touched. Energy coursed across the top of his tongue as he racked his mind for words. His still dead legs dragged behind Hezuz as he pulled him down the hall towards the perfume of burning frankincense.

"I can walk-" Diaz wheezed defiantly as clumps of Hezuz's hair muffled his mouth of its own accord.

"Good-" Hezuz hiccupped back in a light-hearted trill, cloaking the words with dissonance he created within his mouth on purpose. "Because in a moment, you're going to have to *run* like the light of all worlds depended on it... So save it-and enjoy the ride."

chapter forty two

Anukai and Gabryl struggled up onto their feet and saw Kagome over the bodies of the dead Punisher. As they made their way through the throng of Anukai's kneeling blood-soaked people Gabryl felt every white eye on his back as he walked beside her towards Kagome, his breath hitching. Anukai instinctively reached out and looped her right index finger around his left until they got to the front, like she could hear his heartbeat.

The people of Anukai nervously watched the One who made them and the One they called Righteous Kill together for the first time in the clan's history.

Kagome dropped to her knees in front of the child and held out her newest weapon on the ground in front of her, a bewildered smile on her face.

Murmurs of shock danced through the clan as they crawled into pairs, some male and female, others two boys or girls at a time, solemnly holding each other by index fingers, heads dropped as if in prayer.

Anukai grinned as she whispered in tongues to Kagome, wagging a finger at the wild woman on her knees before her. Kagome proudly grinned.

"I figured it was *you* who had taught them how to kill." Anukai murmured.

Kagome blushed fiercely "It came in handy, did it not?"Anukai nodded and Kagome beamed. "Can I keep it?" Kagome asked shyly as her fingers danced along the blade of the sword she had placed at Anukai's feet.

"How could I take it away?" Anukai whispered as she toe-touched the blade laid out before her. "It sure is pretty though-"

"I know!" Kagome crowed. "And look at what they did to the- and the-" she picked it up and flipped it around in her hands.

"Where is your-"Anukai whispered hesitantly.

Kagome looked up.

"Your Guardian returned." she murmured stiffly as she sat back on her haunches, countenance glowing, regaining the composure of an emperor at court.

"...Did you two make up all the way?" the little girl blushed hotly as she asked.

Kagome shrugged her shoulders faintly as a wave of energy slid across her face. She looked at the two exhausted children and remembered they were just that.

Her eyes softened as she took in the details of Gabryl up close for the first time. His brows furrowed as he felt the spider woman watching him. Kagome looked towards the trees.

"You two can go now. No one is left to bother you...but what about them?" Kagome motioned absently towards the clan of Anukai. Anukai looked back at her solemn, gore streaked people.

"They're yours now. Your blood is on them as much as mine. Do as you wish."

Anukai laced her fingers into Gabryl's hand and pulled him towards the Leuce before she called back over her shoulder.

"But send off the fallen one with a proper pyre. His name was.. . Hepa. And... since you taught them to kill, teach them to heal too, for more options. And have them baptize closed that cut of yours so you won't be making more of them until you're ready to take care of more babies."

The little girl and boy disappeared into the Leuce.

chapter forty three

The whitewashed wool habits of the Tryage would have been blinding if the Elohs had not been gazing towards the gilt stenciled floor.

The kneeling ladies were framed by the ornate inner archway and curtains of state that opened onto the shimmering bronze dust of the receiving courtyard. Tiered golden crowns nestled into their variously textured hair. They were demure in a way that cut across the brazen nudity of their torsos under piles of gold chain.

The red light bouncing off the gold chains and the raw beauty of the kneeling women raised hackles on the backs of every neck except for those that surrounded the strangely stoic Third member of the Tryage, positioned on the lowest of the three sedans. Those in the First and Second entourages had no recollection of their own sojourn amongst such visceral loveliness before being released into eternal lives within the cliques chosen for them within the Empyrean.

The sight of them hit First and Second retinues with such force that all 24 of their whirling frankincense decanters crashed to the ground. Smirks spread across the Elohs' cheeks as they inwardly mocked those shocked by such beauty on its knees in front of them.

The incense bearers flung their bodies towards them, hoping that none of their brethren would be smote in broad light by First or Second over objects cherished more than the everlasting lives of those who'd kept them aloft.

Even the beautiful ones were offended by the gorgeousness of the topless women.

The Third Head of Tryage motioned to her retinue to stand down with a disdained wave of her hand. A smile spread across Third's face as she raised up the snarling Edo warrior mask that shielded the beauty of her own countenance and pushed it up into her painstakingly plaited hair before she settled back down onto her cushions for a better view.

A jolt of recognition passed through the bodies of the women as an Eloh with thin dreadlocks that spread out around her as she knelt on the floor was the first to look up and take in the placement of the ornately chromed sedans and supernatural rulers for the fools that they were, full of unnecessary pomp and circumstance in this particular sector, which showcased That they knew they had no right to that which they'd so obviously made the trip to demand, with witnesses in attendance. They didn't decide when purification was complete. The Anannke did. Out of necessity.

Third looked bemused as the battalions of First and Second got into position for proclamations. Third's attendants looked straight ahead, refusing to move as the First and Second Heads of the Tryage council had their attendants crank up their respective sound systems. First Head cleared his throat to get Third's attention.

"Yes, Councilor?" Third responded lazily.
"It seems your *guardians*-" First Head sneered, "aren't in the correct formation to proceed-"

"My people do not answer to your charge, Councilor."

"Then maybe you should give -" snapped Second Head in outright irritation.

"No. Maybe you should pick a different course of action altogether. Unless you're in the mood for completely unnecessary sacrifice." drawled Third Head.

"Oh! And what whispered that into your spirit, Councilor?" First chuckled. "Feminine mystique, perhaps?"

Second sneered as a nervous titter passed through the retinues of First and Second.

"Yes." Third whispered softly. "Then again, what do I know? What, with my feminine hunches and all...Instead, how about this," Third purred. "Consider my men and women here...for amoral support. Lead by example, show Them-" she motioned to the people clustered around her sedan as they collectively looked away from where First and Second stood, "Show how it is done, and what a poor choice they've made by standing in the shadow of my...cause~" Third slurred like the ultimate drag Queen and nestled back down onto the divan inside her birdcage-like chrome carriage.

First and Second snorted and turned back to the task at hand. Tiny chrome-plated bullhorns were buffed, polished and gingerly placed into their greasy palms. Feedback crackled out of the anciently stylized equipment as soon as they were raised to their reptilian lips.

"It is time." Spat out First Head ceremoniously. "We've come for the Kouros-" Static followed the last syllable.

"The Great Fire- the prophesied return of the Master-Builder was witnessed by the entire Empyrean realm. Eons ago. Puryf is Over. " chimed in Second.

There was no response from the kneeling Elohs. Second cleared his throat. "Purification and Preparation should be complete."

"There is much work to be done. It's time to begin Installation." The First and Second Heads of the Tryage said in unison.

The Eloh with the dreadlocks shivered with excitement. Her dreadlocks danced gently out and caressed the perfect leaders within the clutch of demure women.

One of the Elohs on the edge of the throng tilted her head and squinted in confusion at the battalion arrayed on the other side of the courtyard. The fuzzy tendrils of her hair fanned out and twisted into a Mohawk that trailed down her back.

"But are you ...*Pure*?" the Eloh with the Mohawk asked almost rhetorically. Her query set off a landslide of retorts among the clique of Elohs on the ground.

"Are they Pure?"
"They're not *pure*-"
"Definitely not *pure*-"
"Are you *Pure*-?"
"Do you think any of them are *Pure*?"

A confused murmur went through the ranks positioned in front of First and Second Head as Third chuckled.

"You are about to lay siege to the *Purification complex*- on the outskirts of the *Empyrean- the highest high of the highest high.. . and you're surprised- that they're asking you if any of you are purified enough to do it?*" Third muttered under her breath.

She rolled her eyes as she dragged her left thumb across the rest of the fingers on her hand, the closest she had to get to snapping her fingers.

Glyph appeared in a seductively cropped whitewashed wool habit, bowed and presented Third with the halved pomegranate she so genuinely desired to enjoy during the show.

"Ah~ Red Corn. Thank you, Glyph" Third murmured. Glyph's

milky white skin flushed subtly as the weight of Third's stare bounced off the chrome jewelry the beautiful little being had pierced her own face with. The Vestal Elohs continued in the background as First and Second pushed back.

"I repeat! We know you have received the fire! It is time! We are here for the Kouros! This is the Highest High! The Fiery Abode of ye Gods! Of Course we- To even inquire as such is just shy of blasphemy!" First aggressively yelled into his ancient bullhorn.

"But are Any of you *Pure*?"
"He's not *pure-*"
"Blood is all over your hands-"
"Definitely not pure- And you talk of Time?! In this place?"

"You have not even been purified of the conceptual constructs of time yet have the audacity to-"

"You want to steal from This house?!!"
"They dare disrespect *this House-?!*" one hissed rabidly.

"*To dishonor this House-?* " another howled.

"You have the Audacity-" the Mohawked Eloh roared, "to come here ...to *the Pe-ra Purification Complex...*and demand, of all beings, *the Kouros?!* With all the blood you have on your hands? For your paltry, pompously prescribed bureaucratic blood-letting?!"

"You are blind! You have no sense of true Time!" A Vestal cried out to her comrades. "If Any of them were pure they'd have just walked into the sanctuary and retrieved the Kouros themselves!"

"No- the filth on them knew better than to-" an Eloh hissed.

"They knew they'd burst into flames due to their impurities-"

The Eloh with the longest dreads cursed the Tryage softly in the center of the crowd, her syllables throwing kerosene on the already lit spiritual fires of the protective Elohs.

"Retrieval will occur at all costs!" Second yelled, flustered.

A horrified gasp went up from the group of kneeling women. "You choose to insult this house with your arrogance?!" an Eloh seethed.

"You dare threaten to enter this house?! For the Kouros?! Because you think it's TIME?! We will slaughter you ALL for this house!"

"Maybe we should t'ink to purify 'dem, den?" An Eloh with a short halo of fuzzy hair and enough ammunition in her eyes to decimate generations whispered.

The Elohs rose up onto their feet and started to siren call collectively into the mainframes of all the men present like they were the pieces of meat every woman that had stumbled across their earthly paths had once been to them.

Droplets of blood began to splatter onto the ground as the adrenaline-drenched ladies cut away left breasts right in front of the battalions' eyes, readying for battle.

Looks of horror, fear and disgust spread across the faces of those under the command of First Head as "Let's Do this!" rang out belligerently from among those crowded around Second.

"Enough of this nonsense!" snarled Second Head, uncharacteristically taking the lead. "Go get the Kouros!"

The Elohs howled in unison in pools of blood as those assigned to Second Head charged forth.

"Dirty! Polluted! Filthy!Trifling!" The women screamed.

"GO!" First yelled. "Decimate them! Get the Kouros Now!"

The retinue of First Head poured into the courtyard behind Second's gang as the Elohs brandished Scythian blades slick with Eloh blood, ready to protect the purity of the temple at all costs.

chapter forty four

Kagome cocked her head in confusion at the word "babies."

She looked back at the quietly paired off members of the clan as the hairs on the tops of their heads began to undulate up towards the sky like hers.

The last of the two Punishers were burned together with Hepa, the man of Anukai. Kagome sent more heat into the flames, smoke that the people of Anukai roughly inhaled. They entwined legs and cleaved to each other then came apart in the exhaust from the bodies before them, dancing around the fire, re-igniting themselves. Jewelry slicked in black melted in the heat that began to rise up off them in torrents, then froze in the cool breeze in patterns akin to the unhinged exoskeleton of the fallen Punisher.

Kagome looked down at the gash on her stomach and realized in shock that she was flickering in full view, a half-life habit she usually hid. She grunted in surprise as their oiled skins began to flicker too, as if clouds had just passed overhead. They faded in and out of view as she was prone to do and paused, waiting for the next lesson.

She laughed. They looked up at the sound of her laughter and mimicked her, each one's laughter as full-bodied but solely his or her own.

Kagome ran through the crowd like a wild animal that had finally found its kind and dove headfirst into the water. They followed just as wildly, christening her the new head of their family. The twos playfully fused into ones, sliding through streaks of oil, soot and tar before freely disengaging in the waves just because they could.

chapter forty five

Third watched gleefully as the Elohs pounced on the hapless men who forgot the soldiers they were when faced with a ferocious female enemy.

First and Second Head looked on in horror as man after man was ripped apart by the daemonic deities assigned to the front of the Purification House of Pe-ra. The two Leaders cowered in the far corners of their sedans, unable to look away from the carnage as those assigned to them continued to wildly press through the gates only to be slaughtered.

Third grinned and pushed both feet out of her cage. They got splattered as she dangled them evocatively in the air before standing up all the way. White chalk her exposed toes had been dipped in caught wind every time Third wiggled them.

Linen strips snaked up mile-long legs until they disappeared under the jagged hem of Third's re-adjusted whitewashed habit that, though hooded like those of First and Second, had been slashed down to below her navel, exposing cleavage that would have been prized even within the Purification complex.

She shifted and gold chains that were cloaked along the center slash of the habit spilled out as she gingerly balanced herself in an aggressively indifferent stance, smiling as if the blood-curdling screams of the men were familiar music to her ears, listening a few octaves above it for what her routinely disparaged feminine instinct told her was afoot just beneath the surface.

"The Kouros!" screamed Second Head over the wails of his own men and the violently erotic chanting of the swarming Elohs as they tore them limb from limb in his face.

Every droplet of blood spilled by weaponry dried upon contact with the air, creating clouds of bronze dust the courtyard was already full of.

The Eloh with the Mohawk angrily set her sights on Second Head as he attempted to screech orders.

She leapt up in the air, lunging through the brawling crowd towards him on the other side of the Purification gate.

At the moment Mohawk's naked, hennaed and bejeweled feet left the ground towards her target of Second, the coiled Trinidadian twanged Eloh locked onto First and dove underneath her into the fray towards him.

"Filthy!" the Elohs howled.

The once Trini's skin gleamed golden like a Buddha as she berated every man that fell as she fought her way through, raking her hands up through the tiny oxidized coils of her closely cropped hair between punches thrown, hair full of the blood of the fallen except for the bump of it just above her crown as she screamed belligerently.

"You're Filthy! How dare you -How dare you?! You think That you won't have to pay! All of you will pay!"

"I said Push through!!"First Head screamed from the sidelines. "Get the Kouros!"

The bones in Third's gorgeously structured face gleamed in the red light as she stood, bemused by the melee.

A French braid twisted down each side of her head past her bosom, where each braid was left to hang in loose, wild waves that rustled as she stepped all the way down onto the Holy ground.

Securely planted she murmured one word so softly that even Glyph had to lean out of the shadows of the cage towards her to discern whether or not it had actually been spoken.

"Come."

chapter forty six

" Come!"

Inside the purification complex Hezuz froze as the word exploded inside of his head.

"Run!" Hezuz screeched as he yanked a still groggy Diaz the younger down the antechamber, racing against all odds for life after death after rebirth. Due to the escape velocity Diaz snapped awake and slid across the rose petals as they rushed past.

Hezuz refused to look back, his spirit latched onto the word "Come" like a homing beam, not knowing exactly what he was running to, but somehow fully comprehending that it was his destiny.

When they arrived at the courtyard they could see the Tryage glinting on the other side over the backs of the battling beauties. Bodies exploded into coppery dust on impact with the ground between the two gates.

"Dodge through-don't touch anybody until I yell!" Hezuz roared loudly as he roughly threw Vayo Kahn Diaz towards the wake of those felled by Mohawked Eloh.

The two of them cut through the brawling pile of women ripping men apart and returning them to dust, stepping on those insane enough to attack the House of Pera as the men of Second and First shattered left and right upon contact with the Vestal women, falling to the ground in fiery clumps and clouds.

Vayo Kahn bobbed this way and that, leaping over instantly incinerated beings as he tried to catch up with the Mohawked girl ripping men to shreds in front of him, cloaked to the

Vestals he swerved around by nothing but the grace of the illicit torture he'd endured within the complex.

"Now! Now! Now!" Hezuz screamed as he grabbed hold of the Trini-Buddha from behind, not even looking to make sure Diaz followed suit.

Soon as Vayo Kahn Diaz and Hezuz connected with the skin of the Vestals, both warriors spun around in shock as their bodies continued on the paths they'd been set upon, momentarily stupefied by the touch of a man.

The double-pass encoded into their flesh yanked Hezuz and Kahn through the gate without exploding into shards. The un-consecrated atmosphere shook as they touched the Holy ground. The foursome crashed into the rank and file of Third, Hezuz and Vayo Kahn atop the two Elohs they'd freed alongside themselves. The Vestals violently pushed them off before they looked up over their shoulders and realized they had somehow been emancipated.

The Anannke whipped its head up and screamed defiantly from inside the dread-headed Eloh as if she had been wounded, her arc of dreadlocks cascading up into the sky as the membrane between the un-consecrated and the clean ruptured. All the insurgents who still battled on behalf of First and Second spontaneously combusted at the sound of her roar.

The Anannke revealed itself for a split second before the entire scene was erased from the memories of all focused on it. Both sides fell back into their places on opposite sides of the courtyard as much as possible, with First and Second retinues noticeably smaller than they had been when they had initially set out.

All stood awaiting first orders. Elohs waited on their knees fully intact, minus two of their kindred as if it had always been elevating eleven and not the transcending thirteen they'd been trained in.

The Anannke gave one last baleful look towards Third Head as the two Elohs stood up in the midst of Third's attendees who had been instructed to look away from the battle from the beginning.

They clustered around the two freed women who looked back at the gate in happy confusion. The escapees Hezuz and Diaz remained crumpled at the feet of Third, exhausted by both the breakthrough and the pressure of the completely different atmosphere on their restructured lungs.

Third Head took in the one called Hezuz, snorted and looked away, bemused that this was who such a fuss was to be made over. Hezuz wrinkled his nose in disgust, the first taste of smug ambivalence he'd fully experienced in his after-life.

Diaz, more than 120 years younger than he'd been when he'd last left the Empyrean choked down consecrated air beside him.

"Apoc, Apogee, Apex...Rekindle the Fire." Third murmured softly to the three beings closest to her. "Marok, Anad, Yr-is, Soigne -" Third muttered as she climbed back onto her settee. "Refinish the Kouros in preparation for release to the other members of Tryage." They nodded.

First and Second Head looked on in bewildered shock as the Fire-Starter and the Kouros they had made the trek to the complex to forcibly retrieve packed up within the confines of Third's domain, no explanation of how , when or why within the two Tryage Councilors.

There was nothing they could do but bark irritated orders at their own men to begin the exiting processional as they bit their tongues in confused rage.

chapter forty seven

The father did his best to keep his composure as he got out of the van and walked to the back door of the house.

The blue jumper he wore with "Decker" printed on his back was stained with splatters of oil. It felt like a cage. He had been laid off a few days back and the rattling at the top of his chest was the same one that had been there for years. Time ticked away but didn't take any pressure with it as it went.

He looked at the light glaring from the house he had worked his ass off with his wife to buy, that they did everything they could to keep- from throwing parties in ballrooms and the bowels of church basements that the people migrated to once the clubs started getting shut down to selling accessories on the community fair circuit that networked across Cleveland, angelic looking kids in tow who hustled better than the best due to who their parents were.

The father tried not to think about the fact that every light in the house was on. Fear descended, his heart devoured by the demons his own parents had fought off to get more for him and his siblings than they'd ever been able to have, and by what he clairvoyantly knew the mother had bought instead of food for their family on that day's shopping spree. Her shopaholic tendencies threatened the home like another man hidden under the bed.

It made him lash out at what the mother worked overtime for too. They were not "there" yet, but she was hell-bent on looking the part ahead of time.

It made the father insecure, urged him to find a second job on top of the fairs, parties and all else, even when men his shade of Black weren't hired due to hysteria over brothers who claimed their manhood via violence.

As his fury and fear entwined, the father fought against gossip in both the party circuit and amongst brothers on the outskirts of unions about the free-for- all white cops were having against brothers just like them up in New York City, and how it was bound to migrate along the steel town circuit like everything else since nobody was doing anything to stop it.

The men who spread the word were hanging on for dear life, running for cover towards hometowns they had once dreamed themselves out of that had died off in their absence.

Supposedly, many of the targets had been day-workers, between shifts. Others were men up in Central Park, fighting with God, feeling like Job in the dust as they regained their courage and composure in the peace of trees that reminded them of where many of them had come to the city from.

Men who were shot dead and planted with drugs or guns, depending on the cop practicing his aim. In New York, most men were silent, ashamed of so many of their women having to be mom and dad. They just quietly knew not to go into the park. Unless they had given up and had no plans of coming out alive.

The father mourned for the wives who knew that the blue wall of silence built around the events had nothing to do with the kind of men they had known their husbands to be, even as any possibility of passing those untainted memories onto the scores of suddenly fatherless children evaporated like good light disappearing from eyes.

He tried not to be harangued by the thoughts that implored him to "imagine" his little kids without him, how they wouldn't survive- how he had fucked up with the lay-off from the back-up job. That spirit had sunk its teeth into him and made him beg for and get welding work wherever he could.

As his rage fed on itself, he spun on his heels and walked determinedly towards the side of the garage, knowing it was best not to go into the house he loved feeling jobless, even with his main gig steady, until he was calm enough to not fight. Or to win.

He ploughed past the railroad ties he'd used to section off the backyard into zones, past the garden of tomatoes, greens, beans, and roses he had planted and nurtured the last time he'd been laid off, and the patio he had laid the time before that, using the priceless sandstone sidewalks the city had ripped up to replace with concrete. He stopped at the row of garbage cans in the back, near the wild cherry and crab apple trees in bloom that hung heavily in the night sky. The father moved towards the end of the line and lifted the last lid. Because he knew his wife. Crumpled shopping bags from the mall were crushed against the tops of shiny black bags that filled the canister. Attempts to hide what she had done had never gone as deep as they could if she really didn't want him to know.

Sparks shot out of his eyes as he knew he would explode upon seeing her lounging in the house, his offspring hidden off in the cut out of fear. The anger did everything it could to grab hold of him, to lead him into wrath that he promised he would never physically show to the woman who never seemed to love or respect him at all.

His own mother flashed before his eyes to stop him from where he was headed, deep on the other side of life that she was. Tears rose up as he tried to think of anything other than becoming as bad to his wife as his father had been to her.

He looked back towards the house and saw his oldest daughter sitting in the window of the TV room, squinting her eyes to blindly peer out of it, almost catatonic as she waited for him to come into the house and save her from whatever had jumped off that day, to make whatever his wife had done to her not matter.

"I need to build something-" he snapped out of nowhere as he forced himself to start going over what it would take to do just that until he calmed down. Sparks shot out of his eyes again as he ploughed into the side door of the garage, grabbed his welder's helmet and started soldering the bars of protective iron he had all but begged the neighbor of a friend of a friend to build in exchange for enough pay to create the cushion he needed to not worry about the mortgage and tuition for Flower that was almost due.

chapter forty eight

The little girl looked out of her private world at the father as he saw her and turned away, abandoning her.

As flowers from the trees in her backyard floated to the ground she pretended instead that she was still looking up in the forest with Gabryl. Cherry blossoms started to dance down out of nowhere onto them. Gabryl looked up sleepily as they trudged on.

"Your world is crazy-" Gabryl whispered, unaware that Anukai had just checked in at home. "My world is not like this at all-"

"What's the place you hide in like?" Anukai whispered, making every fibre in her body strain to focus on the pressure of his hand against hers so that she could stay and not look at the rivers of embers that had begun to bounce across the stained garage floor and spill out into the driveway.

Gabryl thought for a moment.

He watched the flowers fall from the sky as if the blooms were marking the path back to where they needed to go. "Well," he said pensively, "It's loud...but not normal loud, I mean...I feel like I can hear everything in there, but I hear it all separately, but at the same time, you know?" he asked, hoping she would know because no one else did when he tried to explain.

"Like, each bird or each noise that comes out a bird? Each leaf when the wind blows?" Anukai whispered.

She furrowed her brow trying to follow him as cherry blossoms kept alighting against her forehead. She felt vulnerable by her two worlds crossing out of the blue. Gabryl blushed at her trying to understand and it encouraged both of them.

"Like I hear everything- but not just what the things are trying to say or sing -lots of things have songs that sing out all the time-but, I feel like I hear it all at the same time, what they sing now and what the sound wants to be when its perfect-"

Anukai thought for a moment, trying to wrap her head around it. "What does it look like?"

"Like..." Gabryl looked around in his head then the forest for something to get across what his world was like to him. Anukai watched as he bent over and pressed the side of his face against the moss at the base of a tree, listening.

His eyes flashed at her to join him and she followed suit, trying to hear what he was obviously in tune with. "Close your eyes," he whispered as the world around him broke up into planes and prisms of beautifully faceted light and dark. "Do you hear that?" Gabryl whispered headily as each plane chimed out to him. Anukai strained her ears and suddenly gasped as a very real heartbeat began to pulse out of nowhere.

"Keep your eyes closed! Don't open yet-"Gabryl directed before she could rip open her eyes in shock, groping his hand across until it made contact with hers in the peat. He gently pressed her hand into it and the sound got louder in response to her touch.

"Coooooooool~" She tittered with her eyes slammed shut.

"Okay- now open your eyes, but slowly, and only look at the moss you're on." he said.

As she did her eyes absorbed every pore of the damp moss as it inhaled and exhaled, each breath it took echoing in her ears. It even seemed to sweat against the pressure of its life being seen and heard.

The cherry and crab apple blossoms that floated down in her line of sight seemed to have been created by Picasso, planes of every petal demanding to be the center of attention for as long as they could.

Gabryl grinned as he shyly watched her watching the textures of her world morph into the angular normality of his own strange view. "But in my world," he whispered, "It's like that for everything- all wants to be heard, be a part of some song that is singing me to sleep. That's why I say it's loud. When I look at what's going on. I see a lot of sound."

Suddenly she got very shy as she tried to imagine what she looked like to him if everything around him always looked like this. She imagined the apples of her cheeks became pointed and the inside corners of her eyes turned into straight lines that flashed every time she blinked at him.

"Oh-" Anukai mumbled softly, awed by the completely different place he saw things from as if it almost hurt to imagine it, but in a good way. "Maybe- maybe I- I hear with my eyes and you see with your ears?" She stuttered softly.

"Maybe!" Gabryl laughed and yanked playfully at her hand still pressed into the moss and mud. "Let's go-" He triumphantly yelped, feeling more understood than ever in his whole life. She laughed and jumped up, narrowing her eyes at him as he pretended he was about to run off deeper into the trees under the still falling flowers. Peals of laughter erupted as they both began to jostle in the woods on their way home. Anukai got a ways ahead of him and Gabryl let out a lopsided rebel yell before tackling her.

They came down with a thud next to a beat-up, bloodied and abandoned car seat that stuck up out of the dirt in the middle of nowhere. The color drained from Anukai's face as she looked up into the trees. Hot angry tears began to spill down her cheeks as she tried to figure out what to do, her face twisted up as a confused scream forced itself out.

chapter forty nine

The father worked until long after the motionless child and her violently spastic younger sister should have been sent to bed.

He slid open the glass doors at the back of the TV room and found his wife curled up in a haggard ball, pressed into the corner cabinet on the far side of the destroyed room. The mother's pin-set hair stuck out in tufts over the top of her head, and streaks of dried mascara that had long since been cried off caked on her sallow cheeks.

The little girl sat motionlessly on the couch that was pushed against the wood paneled wall next to the telephone, dead sleep with her eyes all white and wide open at the same time just like the mother slept when she actually could.

In the center of the room sat the car seat that belonged to the girl's younger sister, overturned and soaked with both urine and tiny splatters of blood. In the corner farthest away from both the distraught mother and the sleeping white-eyed older child, Flower howled soundlessly from between the legs of the perfectly square coffee table that had been shoved to the far side of the couch, screaming as if everything in the room was attacking her, like she had been in a fight to the death.

The distressed look plastered across the mother's face was all the father needed to see to know that this had been the state of things the entire time he'd been out begging for work.

"Both of them are gone-" The mother whispered gruffly. "That one hasn't stopped screaming and scratching since I took her out of her chair," she moaned towards Flower, "And your fucking favorite hasn't moved a muscle to help since I picked them up from being watched by Tsunga," she whispered, pointing accusingly at Anukai.

"I don't know- what's wrong-" the mother cried haggardly, "But I know I can't do this anymore. You handle it, you selfish son of a bitch!" she yelled.

She jumped up and ran upstairs before he could respond.

The father looked at both his children helplessly for a moment before moving into action.

chapter fifty

"Anukai, what's wrong? What's going on?" Gabryl whispered into the silence that suddenly descended after she screamed.

He followed her eyes up into the trees. The rubber soles of the untied shoes of a small limp child swung overhead from the branches.

"My sister-" Anukai whispered angrily. "That's- My sister's chair-and she shouldn't be here! This is mine! but she wouldn't-not like- Unless- She did it to her too-" she hissed.

She furiously climbed into the lower boughs of the tree and made her way out onto the branch below the one the still breathing child was lynched from.

She used the sapphire encrusted knife to cut down the toddler who flailed against her as she was slung across her back. The smaller girl dug her teeth and nails into her big sister, drawing blood between howls as Anukai hesitantly climbed back down.

Gabryl looked at the bruised, wrath-filled child as Anukai sat her on the forest floor. She began to lash out like a Tasmanian devil.

"I can't do any of this anymore-" Anukai whispered hoarsely.

"Can't do what?- I don't understand-" He said, alarmed. Anukai whirled around and glared at him, all bets off.

"I Have to go Home-"Anukai said evenly. "I can't play with you anymore! This is what happens when I go away! Go Home, Gabryl! Stay away or it's going to happen to you too!"

"But you can't just leave!" He wailed." We- after everything we just went through?!"

"This isn't real!" Anukai bellowed so loud that everything around them stopped, even her flailing little sister. "I don't even know you! This-" She whimpered, pointing harshly at her little sister, "This is real! This is what is real! And this is my fault because I couldn't get them to believe me! I can't come here and hide anymore or the monster will get my cousins too!"

"I don't understand! What's wrong with your- your-" he stammered.

Anukai looked at Flower, destroyed by guilt. She looked around cagily. "This proves it! Stay away from me Gabryl- or it's going to happen to you too!" Anukai hissed,"like it's happened to them-" she wildly pointed up into the trees.

Gabryl gasped as suddenly the trees overhead were filled with children cowering in the leaves and branches alongside The still hanging bodies of small kids of every creed and color that had been lynched.

"Go away before it happens to you too-" Anukai cried out as she threw down her knife into the moss.

She yanked her sister's hand violently away from the broken car seat the toddler had started to kick and dragged her into the woods.

chapter fifty one

"Anuk- Wake up." The father whispered into the ear of his first child.

She sleepily closed her whited out eyes and then opened them again, her irises self-consciously tightening onto the tired expression on his face.

"I want a wolf dog-you promised-" she whispered groggily, continuing a conversation it hit him they'd had weeks before, before his main schedule had been flipped from third to second shift.

" Ok, I promise, Bayh, now Go get your little sister, Anukai." he murmured as he began to pick up everything that the supposedly autistic child's tantrum had strewn across the den.

Anukai nodded, sleepily crawled across the couch and slid onto the floor in front of the table. Flower mewed soundlessly and swung at her, screams having ripped her throat raw.

Anukai mimicked her and swung back. The toddler pulled back and cocked her head curiously towards her big sister. Anukai mirrored the same action back to her on auto-pilot. The violently beautiful little girl blinked twice at her big sister, desperately trying to be heard, slow then fast. Anukai did the same and then held out her arms and sighed as if she wished to be held.

Flower got excited and mimicked Anukai, who swooped under the table and pulled her out as the father turned the car seat he'd rinsed off in the sink onto towels spread across the kitchen table to dry.

Anukai held her sister up to the father, still sleepy but

triumphant.

Flower panicked momentarily as she racked her head trying to recall who the features in front of her belonged to. She looked back at her big sister, who smiled forcibly at the father and mumbled "Here, Daddy."

The little girl spun her face back around to the man who she could once again place in her stream of consciousness as Anukai's words echoed.

She plastered an identical smile with twice the wattage across her own fat cheeks. Her tongue flipped around in her mouth as it attempted to remember how what she heard felt so she could say it too. A soft frustrated sweat broke across Flower's forehead.

Anukai struggled to keep her arms as strong and stiff as possible so as not to surprise her baby sister with any sudden movements, which could yank her back into the black hole she'd fallen into after being watched by the abusive aunt that Anukai did her best to avoid like the plague.

"Here, Daddy," Anukai whispered again with bated breath as she felt the fight in the little girl, the sound doing its best to squirm out of her. The weary father tried not to cry out over the state of his youngest child who had suddenly and inexplicably stopped talking earlier that year.

"HeDur-e," Flower spat out and looked around at Anukai, who beamed, refusing to cry, knowing that if she did Flower would too. The father swept Flower up into his arms and tucked her head into the crook of his shoulder. She promptly fell asleep.

Anukai looked up expectantly at the father in hopes that she wouldn't disappear from importance to him as soon as she'd done her duty, as was the case most of the time. She slammed herself into his thigh and wrapped her arms and legs around his leg as he began to slowly walk towards the stairs to take them to bed.

"I told them, baby-" The father mumbled, his voice catching as he shifted to handle the added weight of Anukai below on the opposite side of Flower overhead.

"You gone talk when you want to, just like me- you just like your daddy, Flower, nothing's wrong with you, you just don't feel like talking right now-"

chapter fifty two

Gabryl huddled in the clearing.

The wails of the kids overhead began to make him spin out of control as he watched her disappear.

He knelt over and began to throw up peanut butter and rice that reminded him of where home was for him too, bringing back to light everything he had been running from in the first place that had landed him here.

The pressure of what he had been hiding inside erupted as he tried to think about going back.

"It already happened to me-" he whispered to everyone and no one at the same time. "Before the crazy, before I got the-the accident happened after-and I can't tell nobody cause they all hate me for everything else I messed up!" he hoarsely cried out.

He swooned against the sound of his own hidden truth spoken aloud and then burst, screaming at the top of his lungs as he picked up the knife and ran towards the trees nearby, hacking with all his might until they tumbled to the ground one after another like a circle saw had ripped through the grove.

Little kids screamed and jumped as the trees slowly careened towards the floor of the Leuce. Some untied the other ones that had been lynched by the actions of sick adults they had been assigned to.

Gabryl chopped and chopped until the trees were no more than an expanse of destroyed stumps. He collapsed onto the ground and cried until the last of the tears he had in him were gone.

His tears pooled around the stumps of the trees like dead water, a sight he blinked against as he lay in the mud his crying helped create. He hadn't let himself fully cry all of it out of him until then and there.

Gabryl was calmed by how on his side, exhausted, the tree stumps seemed to stick out of his pool of tears like a ladder into something else, something better, that was going to come out of all he had gone through.

Somehow.

He closed his eyes and felt his spirit reach out to the stumps as if they were rungs on a ladder. His soul started to climb, to ascend again for the first time in forever.

When he opened his eyes he was sticky in a pile of dirty sheets on the floor. Back at his Grandmother's house.

When he finally came out of his room, his mother was nowhere to be found.

...and nothing was able to be the same ever again.

The end.

185

ABOUT THE AUTHOR

Author and multimedia artist Angel Brynner has marched to the beat of her
own drum across the arts for over two decades. After formal training with
the vanguard of the menswear industry she helmed her own line of men's
clothing and produced events for the collection in the club scenes of
New York and Tokyo.

She became quietly known for the futuristic cautionary tales back-dropping
her collections, taking over clubs and the guerilla-marketing style she used
to slam her vision into the hearts of her fans. While being sponsored by
Multinational companies desiring audience with her underground tribe, she
returned from Japan to her hometown to press charges against a pedophile
before the statute of limitations ran out.

Cast as a vigilante by a corrupt sex crimes unit for trying to protect another
child from the same attacker, during the media onslaught against
the first brave adults to come forward and press charges against
the Catholic priests that had abused them as children she was hit with a
vision of all those already lost in a sick war on kids no one talked about.

She committed herself & her art to doing something about it.

The grievechronic universe was forged in the fires of imagining the
Armageddon that would erupt through a generation of kids who
had finally had enough abuse at the hands of adults and
banded together under their grievances.
The epic spiritual, metaphysical, and historical implications
of such an event played out on every level- from the hellish norms
that caused it to what would be called heaven by such a broken world-
made her head spin.

Published by Kokopellima Press, each free-standing installment of grievechronic
Is a take-no- prisoners tale.

Alongside AOLAB[the active-art series featuring the multimedia work
that fed Eutaxis, Ecclesia, Exodus, Erebus, Exist and the kinetic collection
of novels that follow them], Angel Brynner's books are the culmination of
an artistic journey many years in the making,
all leading to a mysterious future project entitled **Transcendence.**

Eutaxis. /Grievechronic\...
Angel Brynner
2h 44m

ECCLESIA. /grievechronic...
Angel BRYNNER
3h 3m

EXODUS. /grievechronic\...
Angel BRYNNER
2h 23m

EREBUS./grievechronic\...
Angel Brynner
2h 56m

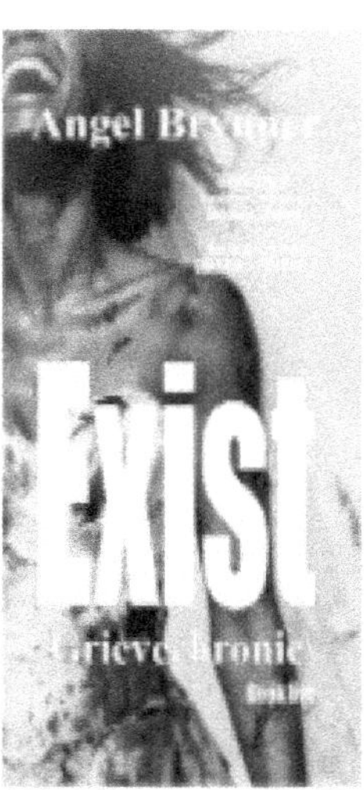

EXIST. /grievechronic\ boo...
Angel Brynner
2h 36m

ESTHESIS. /grievechronic...
Angel Brynner
2h 47m

THE NINTH (& LATEST) ENTRY TO THE / GRIEVECHRONIC \ UNIVERSE

False utopias look like heaven when they exist inside of you, but the spell breaks when you fall. Halcyon days harbor great space for healing if they can stand being held up to the light. The memories we run and hide in may overlap or coincide, but underneath each pleasing space is all that we have yet to face. Hiding bodies to embrace the good is par for the course. But those bones must live again in order to truly break free. The good goes down in spite of what you have to ignore to be grateful for it, but ignoring shit doesn't make anything really go away….and going away only goes so far.

"It looks like Heaven." That may be true. But don't forget what you've gone through

Elysum
before or after the fall may never have been Paradise at all.

ISBN 978-1-950077-83-0
52000
9 781950 077830

Angel Brynner
ELYSUM
/grievechronic\
Now available in paperback
Everywhere.

www.ingramcontent.com/pod-product-compliance
Lightning Source LLC
Chambersburg PA
CBHW070954190726
48292CB00004B/1448